The Club

Takis Würger

Translated from the German by
Charlotte Collins

Grove Press UK

First published in the United States of America and Canada
in 2019 by Grove Atlantic
This paperback edition published in Great Britain in 2020
by Grove Press UK, an imprint of Grove Atlantic
First published in German in 2017 as *Der Club* by Kein & Aber AG

1 3 5 7 9 8 6 4 2

A CIP record for this book is available from the British Library.

Paperback ISBN 978 1 61185 480 0
E-book ISBN 978 1 61185 911 9

Printed in Great Britain

Grove Press, UK
Ormond House
26–27 Boswell Street
London
WC1N 3JZ

www.groveatlantic.com

**GOETHE
INSTITUT**

The translation of this work was supported by a grant from the Goethe-
Institut in the framework of the 'Books First' program.

The
Club

For Mili

The Club

Hans

In the south of Lower Saxony is a forest called the Deister, and in that forest there was a sandstone house where the forest ranger used to live. Through a series of chance events, and with the help of a bank loan, this house came into the possession of a married couple who moved there so the wife could die in peace.

She had cancer, dozens of little carcinomas lodged in her lungs, as if someone had fired into them with a scattergun. The cancer was inoperable, and the doctors said they didn't know how much time the wife had left, so the husband left his work as an architect to stay by her side. When the wife became pregnant, the oncologist advised her to have an abortion. The gynecologist said a woman with lung cancer could still bear a child. She gave birth to a small, scrawny infant with delicate limbs and a full head of black hair. The man and the woman planted a cherry tree behind the house and named their son Hans. That was me.

In my earliest memory my mother is running barefoot through the garden towards me. She is wearing a yellow linen dress and a necklace of red gold.

When I think back to the earliest years of my life it is always late summer. It seems to me that my parents had lots of parties where they drank beer from brown bottles while we children were given a fizzy drink called Schwip Schwap. On those evenings I would watch the other children playing tag and feel almost like a normal boy, and it was as if the shadow that clouded my mother's face had vanished, though that may have been the light from the campfire.

I would usually observe them from a far corner of the garden where our horse used to graze. I was protecting him, because I knew he was afraid of strangers and didn't like being stroked. He was an English Thoroughbred that had once been a racehorse; my mother had bought him off the knacker. If he saw a saddle, he bucked. When I was small, my mother would sit me on the horse's back; later I would ride him through the forest, squeezing my thighs to hold on. At night, looking out over the garden from my bedroom, I could hear my mother talking to the horse.

My mother knew every herb in the forest. If I had a sore throat she would make me a syrup of honey, thyme, and onions, and the pain would vanish. Once I told her I was frightened of the dark; she took me by the hand and we walked into the forest at night. She said she couldn't live with the thought of me being frightened, which troubled me a little, as I was often afraid. Up on the ridgeway fireflies leapt from the branches and settled on my mother's arms.

Every evening, through my bedroom floorboards, I would hear her coughing. The sound helped me to fall asleep. My parents told me the cancer had stopped growing; the radiotherapy she'd had after my birth had worked. I made a mental note of the word "remission," though I didn't know what it meant. Judging by my mother's expression when she said it, it seemed to be something good. She told me she would die, but no one knew when. I believed that as long as I wasn't afraid, she would live.

I never played. I spent my time observing the world. In the afternoons I would go into the forest and watch the movement of the leaves touched by the wind. Sometimes I would sit beside my father on the workbench, looking on as he turned pieces of oak, smelling the aroma of fresh sawdust. I hugged my mother while she made white currant jam, and listened to her back when she coughed.

I didn't like going to school. I learned the alphabet quickly, and I liked numbers, because they were mysterious, but singing songs and making flowers out of cardboard did not come easily to me.

When we started writing stories in German class, I realized that school could help me. I wrote essays about the forest and my mother's visits to the doctor, and these stories made the world a little less strange to me; they allowed me to create

3

an order I couldn't see around me. I bought a diary with my pocket money and began to write in it every evening. I don't know if I was a nerd; if I was, I didn't care.

There were different groups at school: the girls, the footballers, the handball players, the guitar players, the Russian Germans, the boys who lived in the nice white houses on the edge of the forest. I didn't like ball games and I didn't play an instrument; I didn't live in one of the white houses and I didn't speak Russian. At break the girls would come over and join me, and when the boys from my class saw this they laughed at me, so at break time I would often go and hide behind a fish tank, where I could be alone.

On my eighth birthday my mother asked the other parents to bring their children round to our house. I sat quietly in front of the marbled cake; I was excited, and wondered whether the children would become my friends. In the afternoon we played hide-and-seek. I ran into the forest and climbed a chestnut tree. They won't find me here, I thought happily. I stayed up the tree all day; I only came home in the evening. I was proud that no one had found me, and asked my parents where the other children were. My mother told me my hiding place had been too good, and took me in her arms.

All my life my hiding place was too good.

When I was ten, the boys started playing a ball game they'd invented themselves at break, which was so crass and violent that only lunatics or children could have come up with it. The aim was to carry the ball to the other side of the playing field, and you were allowed to use any available means to prevent the other team's players from doing the same. Once, just before the summer holidays, one of the boys was at home with mumps. They needed another player, and asked me if I wanted to join in. Just thinking about it made me panic, because the children sweated and I didn't like other people's sweat; besides, I knew I was terrible at catching. I said no, but they said they couldn't play without me. I ran up and down the grass for a few minutes, pleased at how successfully I avoided holding the ball. A fellow pupil yelled at me to make an effort or they'd all lose because of me. A few moments later an opponent came running towards me with the ball. He was already in eighth grade and was stronger than me. I'd always been small; this boy played rugby for the regional team and he was running straight at me. Quickly I tried to assess the weak points of the body rushing in my direction, then threw my full weight against his right knee and shattered his kneecap. I knelt beside the boy and told him I was sorry but he barely heard me, as he was screaming very loudly. Later he was picked up by an ambulance and his friends wanted to beat me up, so I ran away, climbed a poplar tree and perched in the small branches right at the top. I was never afraid of falling. The children gathered at the bottom and threw lumps of clay at me that they got from a nearby field.

When I came home I saw my father in the workshop, sanding wood. The principal had already called him. I'd been telling myself the whole time that it wasn't that bad—after all, nothing had happened to me—but when I saw my father and knew that I was safe, I began to cry. He held me in his arms and I scratched the dried earth from my shirt.

My father was a bit like me; he was often silent, and I have no memory of him playing ball games. In other ways, he was unlike me; he would laugh loud and long, and this laughter had etched lines on his skin. That night, at dinner, he laid two black cowhide boxing gloves beside my plate. He said that things in life were usually gray, not black and white, but sometimes there was only right and wrong, and when stronger people hurt weaker ones, it was wrong. He said he would enroll me in the boxing club the next day. I picked up the gloves and felt the softness of the leather.

At that time, my parents had a visitor for a few weeks: my mother's half sister from England, who was sitting at the table with us. She hardly spoke any German, and spent most days going for runs in the forest. I liked her, though I couldn't really understand her when she talked. My mother explained that her half sister had a thunderstorm in her head and I should be nice to her, so each day I picked a bunch of marsh marigolds for her down by the duck pond and put them on the table by her bed, and once I stole an apple twice as big as my fist from a tree by the church and hid it under her pillow for her to find.

I hadn't had an aunt until I was eight. Then my grandfather died and my mother found out that she had an older half sister living in England.

She had been the result of an affair, and my grandfather had never accepted her as his daughter. After his death, my mother and aunt had somehow managed to become close, even though they were so different, including in their appearance. My mother was tall and her forearms were strong from working in the garden. My aunt was petite, almost delicate, a bit like me, and she had short, buzz cut hair, which back then I thought was cool.

The evening my father laid the boxing gloves on the table, my aunt went on quietly eating her bread. I was a little ashamed that she had seen me so weak, and surprised by the fact that she didn't seem weak at all, even though she too was small, and had a little patch of scurf on the back of her neck that never seemed to clear up.

Sometimes she would come into my bedroom at night and sit on the floor beside my bed. Now, when I can't sleep, I occasionally look down at the floor and for a moment, if I turn my head very fast, it feels as if she's still sitting there.

That particular evening she spent a long time sitting on the bare floorboards, just looking at me. I was a little frightened, because what she was doing seemed strange. She took my hand and held it tight; her hands were like a little girl's.

She spoke to me in German, better than I expected; her accent was a bit funny, but I didn't laugh.

"When I was your age, it was the same for me," she said.

"Why?"

"No father."

"Was that a reason?"

"It was back then," she said.

We sat like that for a long time. I imagined how terrible life must be without a father, and stroked my thumb across the back of her hand.

"Did the others hurt you?" I asked.

With a sharp intake of breath, she squeezed my hand a little tighter and said something I'd never heard anyone say before:

"If they touch you, come and find me, and I'll kill them."

Alex

He was so naïve. And had these fascinating soft eyes, as if he were always worried, and as if there were a black galaxy hidden in each eyeball. I'll never forget his face that night. He doesn't know it, but back then Hans was one of the few things that kept me alive.

On one of the days when the sun didn't rise I saw him in the garden, sitting on the grass, and I went and sat next to him.

"How are things?" I asked.

His black hair was thick, like an animal's. He sat there beside me, and I sensed in him the same heaviness that numbed me by day and kept me awake at night.

"I'm sad, Aunt Alex," he said.

I would have liked to put my arm around him, but didn't dare. For a long time I thought that if I got too close to people they might catch my bad thoughts, like Spanish flu.

He was like the water in the forest, gentle and quiet. I had to look after him. My sister couldn't; she was raising him with kisses. What good did it do him if she kissed away his tears when the children at school wanted to beat him up?

Sometimes I would secretly watch him at boxing training. I would stand behind the door to the gym and watch through the yellow-tinted glass. I never wanted children, and I wouldn't have been a good mother; nonetheless, when I saw this boy standing between the dangling punch bags, trying to find the strength to hit them, I was touched. He would be able to protect himself if someone showed him how.

Hans

Evening light slanted across the gym; the punch bags hung on chains suspended from the ceiling. After training I would sit in the car, steam rising from my shirt. My father would have been watching, and we would both sit there in silence.

I could see that he was happy; at least that's what I thought at the time.

Four times a week he would take me to training and watch. Afterwards my mother would cook us fried potatoes with onions and gherkins, which she called a "farmer's breakfast." When I was grown up I made it myself a couple of times, but it didn't taste the same.

A few weeks later the boys at school wanted to beat me up again. This time, too, I ran away, but then I thought better of it and stopped. I turned and raised my fists, the way my boxing coach had shown me, the right one beside my chin, the left at eye level in front of my head. No one attacked me.

I trained until the capsules in my knuckles ached. To me, boxing was different from other sports because no one expected me to enjoy it, and I could be alone with my pain, my strength, my fear. I was closer to other boys when I was boxing than I had ever been before. When we practiced sparring at close range I could smell their sweat and feel the heat coming off them. It bothered me, and to begin with I often felt nauseous, but I got used to it. Now, when I look back at that time, I think I only became able to tolerate other people when I started to fight them. I preferred to box at a distance, from long range, keeping my opponent at arm's length.

At thirteen I fought my first match and lost on points. I remember that, though I don't recall my opponent. My father was at the ringside. In the car he kissed my knuckles and said he'd never been as proud of anything as he was of me. I remember that clearly.

One November day, when I was fifteen, we were driving to Brandenburg for a tournament. On the way there, on a bridge over the Havel just outside Berlin, there was a sheet of ice on the road. Our car skidded on the bend and slid into the crash barrier. My father got out and walked towards the traffic coming up behind us so no one would plow into the car with his son in it. I stayed in the passenger seat and was afraid. In the rearview mirror I saw a cement truck with a flashing sign on the windshield that said HANSI. The radiator of the truck hit my father and split him in two. The cement truck was slightly dented. I don't remember the funeral, or the months that followed.

Six months later I found my mother lying in the garden. She was outside because I'd asked for chives to sprinkle over my scrambled egg that evening. Her movements were slow; there was a glint in the corner of her eyes, and beside her lay a little basket of the fresh chives she had cut for me. She gazed at me. I thought she looked beautiful.

I called the ambulance, then sat beside her in the grass and listened as the rattle in her lungs grew fainter. Her grip on my hand remained firm even when her breath fell silent. The autopsy found that she had died from a honeybee sting; the venom had triggered anaphylactic shock.

The coffin was made of cherrywood. My father had built it years earlier in accordance with my mother's wishes and had carved flowers all over it. People threw earth into the grave with a little trowel. My mother's half sister was wearing a white dress; she reached down, took some earth in her hand and dropped it onto the coffin. That made an impression on me. I thought of how my mother used to kneel in the garden picking strawberries, and I too took a handful of earth.

My father had died because I wanted to box in Brandenburg. My mother had died because I wanted chives on my scrambled egg. For a few days I waited to wake up from this nightmare, and when that didn't happen I became filled with a darkness so overwhelming I'm astonished that I survived.

After the funeral my aunt spoke to me in English; she was crying, and her left eyelid fluttered with every word. I didn't understand her. I couldn't cry; I wanted to scream, though I had never screamed before.

There was a cross behind the altar in the church. I went to look at it. The Jesus who hung there looked indifferent. I took off my suit jacket and punched the church wall with my fists until my left metacarpal broke at the base of the little finger.

Alex

Goya went deaf in early 1792. He'd had a fever, and became so ill that he lost his hearing. Afterwards he moved to a villa outside Madrid, where he painted fourteen pictures on his dining-room and drawing-room walls. Goya didn't name these pictures. He is assumed to have painted them for no one but himself. They are known as the *Pinturas negras*, the *Black Paintings*. I think it's a beautiful name.

Dark, disturbing works, full of violence, hatred, and insanity. They're works of genius, but they're hard to look at. One of the paintings depicts the god Saturn devouring his son because of a prophecy that one of his progeny would overthrow him. Some say Goya's deafness made him go mad. There is madness in the eyes of the god in that picture.

Is it part of my illness when I feel that pictures speak to me, or do other people feel the same?

Madness was already part of my life when my sister died. It's easy for me to admit this, because it explains a lot. The doctors didn't call it that; they talked about dissociation and trauma, but I know that I was grappling with madness. I had to vanquish it alone. If I'd taken Hans in I would have destroyed us both. The dark thoughts would have infected him. I knew what it was like to grow up without a stable family, and I couldn't have provided that stable family for him. At boarding school he was safe.

They broke Goya's picture of Saturn off the wall, and now it hangs in the Prado. Everyone raves about the eyes, but they're not the crucial thing. The crucial thing is a section that was painted over because people would have been too distressed by it. I've examined that painting very closely. Under the dark patch that covers the god's nether regions you can make out that Goya painted him with an erect penis.

I would have dragged the boy with me into the abyss. I wasn't ready yet. I wasn't myself.

Hans

Our horse was taken away, and I was sent to boarding school. My aunt became my legal guardian; I thought she would come and fetch me, but she didn't. I didn't dare ask her why she decided not to. She sold our house in the forest and used the money to pay for the Jesuit school. In the brochure it said: "Order and decorum in everyday life are essential, along with respectfulness and the willingness to help one's fellow man. We ensure that each individual pupil is guaranteed a well-regulated boarding school environment in which he is motivated and willing to learn." This sentence made me uneasy.

My suitcase contained five pairs of trousers and five shirts, underwear, socks, one of my father's woolen jerseys, my mother's necklace, a hat, a twig from the cherry tree, my brown diary with the unlined pages and the black cowhide boxing gloves.

Johannes Theological College was situated on the slopes of the Bavarian Forest; it looked to me like a knight's castle, with its towers and crenellated walls. For centuries it served the Jesuits as a place of retreat, and in World War II some members of the resistance group known as the Kreisau Circle met here to plan the murder of Adolf Hitler.

When I saw the boarding school for the first time, the sun was shining through the fir trees and the mountain breeze blew Italian warmth into the countryside, but this was just part of the deception.

On my first day at boarding school I visited the principal's study. He was a friendly young man; we sat at a table covered with a linen cloth. I gripped the cloth under the table and thought of my mother's yellow dress.

The principal said he understood if I needed time, but I knew that he didn't understand a thing. He had a wart on his forehead and smiled, although there was no reason to do so. I wondered why he was taking notes.

At Johannes Theological College every pupil had to give a urine sample on Monday morning, which was tested for narcotics.

The pupils were either the sons of rich businessmen or boys who had taken so many drugs their parents thought the monks would be better equipped to deal with them.

Twelve monks lived in the castle; eleven taught, and one was a cook. His name was Father Gerald and he was from Sudan. I liked him because he was different and had a sad smile. Father Gerald didn't talk much; when he did, it was in English, and his voice sounded deep and foreign. When he cooked, he boiled everything for too long.

On the first day I went to the washroom and looked at the basins hanging all along the wall. I counted them: there were forty. Everyone here seemed to live on an equal footing. That night a few of the pupils threw balls of paper at me, chewed into compact projectiles. I pretended not to notice. Later they stole my pillow. After a few weeks, an older boy slapped the back of my neck with the flat of his hand as I was queuing in the dining hall. I felt my ears turn red. I grinned, because I didn't know what else to do; it only hurt a little. The boy stood behind me and asked loudly if I missed my mama, and if that was why I always whimpered in my sleep at night. I turned and punched the boy in the face with a left hook. The impact made a sound like the opening of a jam jar.

Father Gerald saw it all, and grabbed me by the arms. I thought I'd be expelled from the school, and I was glad, because I hoped that meant I'd be able to go and live with my aunt in England. I didn't know that the school needed the money because some of the monks had invested in Icelandic high-tech companies and had lost a lot of the foundation's capital. Also, the boy I'd hit was a troublemaker and the principal was secretly glad that he was in the sick bay. He made me reorganize and clean the wine cellar as a punishment.

After the punch-up the other children avoided me. I let them copy my math homework, and once, after spending days summoning up the courage, I asked if anyone wanted to play hide-and-seek in the forest. I resolved not to run as far away this time, but the children weren't interested in me and said playing hide-and-seek was childish. Perhaps I need to tell them more about myself, I thought, so I told them how oranges tasted of adventure, and how the soft hair at the nape of girls' necks sometimes looked like candyfloss. They just jeered at me.

One of the monks told me I shouldn't pay any attention to the fact that I was poorer than the other pupils. He gave me a Bible with a silk bookmark indicating a passage of Job in the Old Testament: *the Lord gave, and the Lord hath taken away; blessed be the name of the Lord.* I climbed the church tower and flung the Bible into the Bavarian Forest.

I stayed sane because I was able to spend time alone, which for the most part I enjoyed. I read and went for walks in the forest and tried to identify the birds. I became good at that.

Once, when we had been studying the Book of Genesis in religious education yet again, I thought about which hundred people I would save if the world were about to end. I couldn't think of one hundred people who deserved to go in the ark, but I would have filled the boat anyway, with Father Gerald's extended family. That wasn't what preoccupied me, though. What first troubled me, then filled me with sadness, was the realization that there was no one who would let me onto their ark.

I missed my parents, and I missed the house, the smell of the old floorboards, the furniture my father had made, every corner of the cool walls that held a memory for me. It was like the hunger I used to feel when I wasn't allowed to eat before one of my boxing matches because I had to lose two kilos to reach my weight class. The hunger was a hole I felt in my stomach. The loneliness was a hole I felt in my entire body, as if all that was left of me was an empty husk.

To begin with, my aunt wrote me a letter once a month, in English, in which she mostly told me what was happening at her university. I wrote her long letters about the noises in the dormitory, and the other children, and how I dreamt about my father without a face, but she never responded to this.

The wine cellar I was supposed to reorganize as a punishment was long and cool. Every now and then I threw a few punches in the air. I hadn't asked if I could carry on boxing at boarding school. The gloves were stowed in the suitcase under my bed. I took off my shirt and shadowboxed until the sweat poured from my fists, dripping onto the bottles as I punched.

A shadow moved in the darkness. "Your left is too low."

I stared at the monk. I'd be in trouble now. Father Gerald in his black cassock was almost invisible in the dark of the cellar.

"You drop your left," he said. He held up his right palm like a punch mitt. Seeing his stance, I knew that Father Gerald was a boxer. I hesitated for a moment, then stretched out my left arm and touched the pale-pink palm with my fist.

Father Gerald took a step back and raised both hands. I punched: left, right. The priest described a hook. I ducked. From one combination to another the pace of the punches increased. The sound of fists on palms echoed through the wine cellar, the rhythm of a language that needed no words. At the end Father Gerald let me hit three hard punches with my right. He winced, then laughed.

"Call me Gerald."

"Hans."

It was the first time in ages that I'd spoken because I wanted to.

"Thank you," I said.

The next day I put my boxing gloves in a rucksack and took them with me to the wine cellar. Father Gerald had brought two small, hard sofa cushions; he had used a filleting knife to cut holes in them for his hands. They were the softest mitts I would ever hit.

"Let's go," said Father Gerald.

Hans

The months at boarding school passed me by. When I wasn't in the wine cellar I spent a lot of time sitting in the tower next to the chapel bell, because there I could read undisturbed. Sometimes I would gaze at the edge of the forest and dream about how I would start a better life there when I finished school. Every hour a monk would pull on the bell rope down below, the bell would ring, and I would press my hands to my ears.

Then I received a letter with two mauve stamps displaying the profile of Queen Elizabeth II. My name was written on the envelope in small letters, a soft, round handwriting I knew belonged to my aunt. Her letters weren't affectionate, but they still made me happy because they were the only ones I received.

Twice, early on, I had spent the holidays with Alex in England, but she had worked all day and when we sat at table in the evening, drinking warm beer, she had cried a lot. She put beer in front of me on the table every night, as if that was normal, and apologized when she cried.

I didn't visit her again after that. I spent bank holidays and the whole of the summer with the monks. At boarding school I had a library full of books, and boxing lessons with Father Gerald; it wasn't much, but it was better than an aunt who made me feel like the loneliest person in the world.

This letter was written on pale brown paper. It was too short, and in English.

Dear Hans,

I know: I haven't written to you for a long time. I hope you are happy. I would like to invite you to visit me in Cambridge. There's something you might be able to help me with. I will take care of your travel expenses.

With best wishes,

Alex

I read the letter again and again, and each time I got stuck on the sentence *There's something you might be able to help me with*. I didn't have many qualities that might be helpful to other people. Perhaps I was good at listening, because I spoke so little. Father Gerald said I was a talented boxer, but it had been a long time since I'd stood in the ring. My school grades were good, but that was mainly because I worked hard. I studied because I preferred being with books to being alone. My only friend was a monk from Sudan, but he was twice as old as me so he didn't count, or that's what I thought at the time.

There was hardly anyone who would have missed me if I'd jumped off the church tower. To me, the strangest thing was that I never felt any desire to jump. I just wanted a friend I could have a beer with.

I remembered my aunt's white dress. I'd never had a long conversation with her, and I'd known, ever since the night when she'd sat by my bed in my room, that she was different somehow.

I'd Googled her once, after my mother's death, and read her CV on the website of a charity she supported, which helped disadvantaged children. I could remember most of it: Alexandra Birk, born in Stoke-on-Trent in the north of England, studied History of Art at Cambridge, did her PhD somewhere in New York, became a lecturer at Cambridge at just twenty-eight. In the summary of her career it said that when she was fifteen she'd come second in a national painting competition, and that the awards ceremony had been the first time she'd ever set foot in a museum. She was an expert on eighteenth-century European art and ran ultramarathons in her spare time, races more than forty-two kilometers long.

The evening I got the letter I took a blanket up the church tower and thought about how often I had wished my aunt would drive up one of the winding roads, come and fetch me and take me in her arms the way my fellow pupils' parents collected their children at the start of the summer holidays. She would fetch me and take me with her on an adventure.

Up in the church tower I remembered her hard face, her narrow cheeks, not an ounce of fat upon them. Alex Birk had never taken me in her arms, not even at the funeral.

The night was cold and the wind buffeted the church tower, making the pewter bell hum quietly.

* * *

Two weeks later I was sitting in a room in Chapel Court of St. John's College, Cambridge, looking past Alex at a picture on the wall behind her. I wondered whether old paintings got darker with the years or whether they'd been painted that way.

The college courtyards looked as if their cobblestones had been laid in the Middle Ages, which they probably were. Over the centuries the hard leather soles of thousands of students had trodden down every corner of the stones, leaving them soft and round. I'd leaned against a wall for half an hour, watching the students; they looked like my fellow pupils at boarding school. I couldn't see anything that connected them or suggested that they were somehow special. There were young black people, white people, and Asians; students in loose cotton trousers, short skirts, or suits; students carrying rucksacks, briefcases, or cloth bags, or carrying their books in their hands. At first I thought there was no such thing as a typical Cambridge student; but then I noticed that the men in particular held their heads a little higher than I was used to. They seemed to have a slightly clearer sense of who they were.

Alex's study was paneled with dark wood; her white shelves looked as if they were from IKEA. They were packed with books that Alex had lined up so their spines were exactly level with the front of the shelf. Every surface, every corner was scrupulously clean: there was no dirt in this room, not even dust.

23

We had greeted each other with a handshake, like strangers, which was basically what we were.

As usual, I didn't say anything at first. Alex regarded me without speaking, as if she were searching for something in my eyes.

"It's . . . really beautiful here," I said.

"Lots of people say it's the most beautiful college."

"Yes, such . . . such beautiful stones."

I thought the colleges all looked the same: ancient, and hidden behind thick walls.

Alex went on looking at me, not once averting her gaze.

"Do you know who founded the college?"

"Lady Margaret Beaufort," I said, pleased that I knew. I'd walked around the courts and had read it on a stone plaque.

"And do you know how?" asked Alex.

I shook my head and looked out of the window. Outside some tourists were taking photos of each other on their iPads in front of an apple tree.

"Lady Margaret died in 1509, after dining on swan, or so they say. Not long before, a friend of hers, Bishop John Fisher, had asked her to found a college in Cambridge. Fisher must have been a bold man, or possibly just a deceiver. In any case, he got hold of Lady Margaret's will after her death and added—in black ink—that part of her legacy should be invested in the new St. John's College."

Alex paused for a moment.

"Why am I telling you this?" she asked.

I shrugged.

"Because sometimes deception is a way to achieve something good."

I wriggled my toes inside my shoes; I sometimes did this when I was nervous. Perhaps I'd misunderstood, I thought. I didn't like the sound of "deception."

"Hans, I want you to study here. You'll be given a place and a scholarship, I'll see to that. In return, you'll become a member of a club. I don't suppose you've ever heard of it. You'll become a member of the Pitt Club."

She looked at me and waited for a reaction.

"Sorry," I said, for no reason. Alex didn't respond.

The tourists in the courtyard were now photographing each other jumping in the air. It seemed the iPad shutter release was too slow; the women kept jumping over and over again.

Alex went on talking. She was calm.

"Your mission is to find out what the university boxers get up to there. You do still box, don't you?"

"Sorry, I don't understand what you're talking about," I said.

"I know it sounds strange. It's a club for young men here at the university who think they're better than everyone else."

"A club?"

"A kind of student fraternity. Almost two hundred years old."

"And they're all boxers?"

"No, not only. I think they're a sort of club within the Club. It's only a suspicion. A lot of important people have boxed for the university."

"What do you suspect?"

"I can't tell you," she said.

"Why not?"

"You'd ask the wrong questions at the Club."

"You want me to move to England and you won't tell me why?"

"You could put it like that," she said.

I tried to stay calm by staring at the painting on the wall. It didn't help.

"That's insane," I said.

"I'd be careful how you use that word."

"Why would I move here?" I asked.

"It's the best university in the world."

"But it all sounds completely insane."

"You'll be given a new name so no one finds out who you really are, or that we're related."

I smiled. I didn't know why, but I couldn't stop. "What's all this about?"

"It's about a crime, Hans. I need your help, because I have to solve a crime."

I said nothing for a while. "A crime," I murmured eventually.

"At the Pitt Club," said my aunt.

"What about the police?"

"They can't help us."

"Alex, sorry, but is this all some kind of joke that I don't understand?"

She looked serious. "I hardly ever joke."

I looked outside, where one of the tourists had quickly pulled up her top and was letting herself be photographed bare breasted in front of the apple tree. Her breasts were pointy.

I stammered, "Can I think about it?"

"Of course."

At that moment the whole world seemed to be upside down. Alex held out her hand. This time I was glad we didn't have to hug.

I walked swiftly out of the room. In the court I asked a porter why people were taking photos of themselves in front of the tree. The porter, who was wearing a bowler hat, said tourists were always getting it wrong: they thought this was the tree Isaac Newton was sitting under when the apple fell on his head. The real tree, or rather a scion of it, was outside Trinity College, just up the road.

I walked around town for a while, having a look before I headed to the station. I wandered through college courts and contemplated the oriel windows, the stately libraries, the ancient stone walls. Alex had explained to me on my first visit how this place worked: there were autonomous colleges in which the students lived, and all the colleges together constituted the university. It sounded complicated.

*   *   *

Every single pebble seemed more important than everything I had ever thought or touched in my life. Some colleges looked like little castles and the porters in front of them like guards. King's College had a chapel the size of a cathedral; behind it, a white cow grazed in a meadow. Daffodils were growing in the court of Gonville & Caius, and I listened to a tour guide who was saying that ramps had been put on all the steps so Stephen Hawking could move around freely. Outside the gate of Trinity College a porter in a purple-lined cape was standing guard. When I tried to go through the gate into the inner courtyard he stood in my way and said something I didn't quite catch. The lawns all had little signs reminding you that you were not allowed to walk on them.

It was getting dark, a light fog lay over the city, and there was a smell of Sunday roast. I decided to take a last look at St. John's, where lots of students seemed to be streaming towards a specific place. Earlier they had all looked different; now almost all of them were wearing a black gown over their suit, shirt, dress, or jersey, which made them seem much older and much more important. They looked a bit like wizards. They were a community. I followed them as they entered St. John's College Chapel, which was large and imposing with colorful windows and a vaulted ceiling. The choir began to sing, a high, foreign-sounding anthem. I saw the students whispering in each other's ears, saw how happy they looked. Nobody was alone.

* * *

When I landed in Munich I checked my e-mails and found a message from Alex. It consisted of just one sentence, with no salutation or greeting: *The artist must know the manner whereby to convince others of the truthfulness of his lies. —Pablo Picasso*

I didn't reply.

Alex

Papers belonged in files and on shelves; the laptop went in a drawer. The desk had to be left empty. Order was essential.

Hans would do it. He had grown up; he'd become a good-looking young man. He would do it, though he didn't know it yet. I'd seen him as a child, standing in the boxing gym trying to muster his strength, just as he was trying to muster his courage today. He would come.

At home I drank a glass of whisky and smoked three cigarettes in my little front garden where I grew flowers and a few herbs for the kitchen. The roses needed pruning. I double-locked the front door and went to a room that had nothing in it but my bed.

It had been difficult to find a company that made blinds that kept out every chink of light. I'd had a specialist brought over from Dublin. I closed the bedroom door and lowered the blinds. This is how dark it must be in hell, I thought, exhaling slowly.

Lying in bed, I thought of Charlotte and wondered whether there was any such thing as coincidence. As always, I loosened a strap that was looped around the right side of the bed, put my wrist inside and pulled the loop tight so that the hand couldn't get at my neck in the night.

Hans

I spent the months leading up to my final exams in the library and studied so hard that I often succeeded in forgetting about Alex. Sometimes I would think about the black gowns and the life I could have if I went to Cambridge. I took my school-leaving exams, specializing in Physics and Math. At the graduation service I sat in the back row next to Father Gerald. Alex hadn't come. I'd written her a letter telling her the date. I hadn't responded to her offer.

At the service, one pupil sang Wagner's *Song to the Evening Star* and then a song by the pop singer Herbert Gröne-meyer. The principal was sitting in front of me and I saw him make a note on his pad reminding him to tell the choirmaster that music like that had no place in church. In his speech he quoted the Gospel according to St Mark and talked about Lothar König, a Jesuit priest and former Johannes Theological College pupil who had fought in the resistance against the Nazis. The principal said Father König should be an example to us; he had been active in the anti-Nazi underground right up to the end of the war. Personal initiative and humanitarian thinking were the values Johannes Theological College stood for.

In the school library was a book that described the lives of all the school's well-known graduates. I'd read the chapter about Lothar König when we were snowed in one winter. König had planned to blow the back of Hitler's head off with a sniper rifle at a party conference in Berlin, but he was betrayed, and had to spend the rest of the war hiding in a coal cellar.

After the service I hugged Father Gerald, picked up my suitcase and left the school on foot. My fellow pupils drove past me in their cars as I walked down the winding road to the village. It felt as if the muscles in my throat were relaxing; they'd been seized up for so long I'd started to think it was normal. At last the tears came. I didn't wipe them away; I didn't care that my fellow pupils saw me crying and honked their horns.

Her car came up the road. She was driving a rental car, a little one, and I couldn't have cared less about that because she was here to pick me up; she was late, yes, but an hour's not important when you've been waiting for three years.

Alex was wearing a black leather jacket and a silk scarf. She stopped beside me on the country road and opened the passenger door.

"Congratulations, dear Hans," she said.

"You came," I said.

We drove along the country road. I didn't know what to say. I was enjoying the companionable silence, and jumped when Alex spoke.

"Your course starts at the beginning of October."

"What?"

"I've arranged it."

For a moment I wanted to be angry, but actually I was glad.

"Why me?" I asked, when I realized she was even better than me at saying nothing.

"I trust you," said Alex. After a while she added, "I need you more than you can imagine."

I was eighteen years old, and I'd spent the past three years dreaming of an adventure that would save me.

"All right. I'll do it," I said, quietly but clearly.

Four and a half weeks before my studies began I flew to England with Alex, and on the very first day I regretted coming too early, because there was no one in college apart from the graduate students and a few Pakistani undergraduates who spent their time flying model helicopters across Chapel Court. My room was small, the ceiling was low, the window was drafty, and the fireplace was bricked up.

Alex only came to visit me in my room once in the weeks before the start of term. She shook my hand and said she knew a woman who would help me, a graduate student, and that I should meet her on the first Thursday of term at six p.m. on the bridge behind Trinity Hall.

"What's her name?" I asked.

"She'll tell you," said Alex, and left.

Later I wrote her an e-mail and asked if she felt like going for a walk. The first few days I'd thought she might show me around town and invite me for a beer, but I realized now that had been a childish hope. I didn't get an answer.

The following Thursday I was at the meeting place twenty minutes early. I walked onto a bridge over the Cam that smelled of algae and leaned on the balustrade. It left green marks on my jacket, but that didn't bother me.

The woman was wearing a hoodie with cutoff sleeves. I'd seen her from a distance; I could tell she knew who I was and was waiting for me.

She walked past twice behind me over the bridge. I stared into the water and pretended I hadn't noticed because I didn't dare speak to her.

"Hans?"

Her voice was gentle. I turned around. She smelled of soap and something else; mints, possibly. She had long eyelashes and blonde hair. I thought her cheeks looked as if they would have dimples when she laughed, but she didn't laugh.

She wasn't at all fat, but she was soft all over; at least that was my impression. I imagined that even her collarbones would feel soft. She had been spared the sharp features often found among the British upper classes.

"Let's walk a bit," she said.

I felt uncomfortable because I didn't know who she was. The sun would soon be going down. We walked down side streets hemmed in on both sides by thick college walls. The walls were so high that the streets were always in shade, even during the day. She led the way, along a route that took us past the tourists and back onto the banks of the Cam. Her sleeveless top kept shifting slightly, and I couldn't help staring at her shoulders from behind. She was muscular, as if she were accustomed to hard manual labour.

When we got to the fields outside the town and were alone, the woman began to speak. She sounded as if she had learned what she was saying by heart. Her first sentence was "I can help you get into the Pitt Club." She spoke without stopping, snatching breaths between words. She said a member had to nominate me. This member had to write my name in a book in the entrance hall of the Club, where other members could sign for me. Finally a committee would vote on who was to be admitted. I tried to take an interest in all of this.

She looked at my trainers, and said it was important that I try to be like members of the Club. And I had to learn how members behaved with women. She would arrange for me to be invited to one of their parties, and—

I stopped her. "Why do you have these shoulders?"

She was standing a few paces ahead. She was a bit taller than me. I looked her full in the face for the first time. She wasn't wearing makeup.

"What?"

I stared at the ground and said nothing.

"What I've just told you is more important than my shoulders. Do you understand? The people in this club are criminals," she said.

"Yes, I understand."

"I hope you do."

"What have they actually done?" I asked.

"Alex says I shouldn't tell you."

"How do you know Alex, anyway?"

"She's supervising my PhD."

"And how do you know about the Club? I thought they were all men?"

Her mouth softened. She was silent for a moment.

"You've had your three free questions for the month," she said.

I didn't know how to respond to that.

After a while she said, "That's Kingston," and pointed behind me to a black horse on the other side of the meadow.

"I want to know what I'm doing here," I said. But the young woman didn't answer me; she climbed through the planks of the fence around the paddock.

"Don't be afraid," she said.

I didn't like it that she was treating me like a child. And I didn't like the idea of going into the meadow, but I followed her because I didn't want to look like the coward I was. The horse pawed at the ground with its hooves. I stopped a few meters away.

"If you show that you're afraid, she'll bite," she said, and slapped the mare on the flank. The horse flattened its ears and walked towards me. I stood still while it snuffed my hair and hands. Then I walked backward towards the fence.

"You're afraid, laddie, much too afraid," the woman called.

We walked side by side along the river, accompanied by the smell of wood smoke: people used pine logs to heat the houseboats moored nose to tail along the banks of the Cam. Back in town we could see the tower of our college chapel; it was taller than everything else.

"You'll need to be braver than you were this evening."

I didn't answer. It surprised me that she spoke of bravery. She looked as if she were always about to burst into tears, yet at the same time there was something so determined about her. It's always hard to read the faces of people you've only just met, but I could tell that this woman was afraid. After all, I knew about fear.

"I guess I ought to thank you for helping me," I said.

We both nodded.

"Thank you," I said. I shook her hand and said I wanted to walk a bit longer. I turned and headed back the way we'd come. After a few meters I called, "What's your name, by the way?"

"Don't get lost on your walk, laddie," she replied.

I could feel her watching me for a while as I walked away.

When I got to the paddock I climbed through the fence. The horse came towards me and in a single movement I sprang onto its back. I sat there and took a few breaths; I could feel its heart beating, half as fast as mine. For a moment I was worried that I might have forgotten how to ride, because I hadn't sat on a horse's back since my mother died. I rode for a while, after which I no longer knew whether to be worried or grateful that I had come to this place. I slid off the animal's back.

My feet left prints in the grass, and the dew soaked my trainers. Walking home, I thought about the fact that I still didn't know her name.

Charlotte

I could feel the effect of the two whisky sodas I'd had in the pub. I sat on a bench in the college garden, taking deep breaths of night air to sober up.

After we'd said goodbye I'd followed this boy, Hans. He'd come from Alex, which meant he wasn't a danger; and he really wasn't more than a boy, nineteen at most. I crept along behind him in the dark; I felt a bit foolish, but I wanted to know what he was doing out on his own in the fields. So I stood behind a tree near the paddock and watched him leap onto Kingston's back. He'll fall off, I thought. Kingston never lets anyone ride her except me. When I saw him gallop, it was the first time I thought things might turn out all right in the end. A moment later the thought was gone.

Hans

A month after the start of the academic year I walked through the front door of the Pitt Club and hoped no one there would find out who I was or why I'd come. I'd read online that Prince Charles was alleged to have said he'd learned more in a night at the Pitt Club than in three years at Trinity College. I had no interest in Prince Charles.

On that first visit to the Club I tried to impress every little thing upon my memory. The faces, the burn marks in the carpet, the gnu skull on the wall. Huge white lilies stood in vases in corners. An invitation had materialized in my pigeonhole at the start of the week. I thought about the blonde woman who had said she would help me. Perhaps she would be there too. She was strange, but I hoped she would come. This was the first party I'd been to in my life; it felt wrong that I wasn't here voluntarily, and had only been invited because an unknown, nameless woman had arranged it. It had taken me six attempts to tie my bow tie.

Behind me a young man with round shoulders and a handsome face was gently nudging me towards the bar. This was Billy, a mechanical engineering student with shaggy hair and an incipient paunch; he was drunk and smelled of sweat, and generally looked rather unkempt. I'd met him three weeks ago at the boxing gym, and had nodded at him during one of the initial training sessions. He'd been waiting for me afterwards by the bike stands.

"Hi, I'm Billy."

"Hi."

We cycled part of the way back together without speaking. I was happy to have someone to ride with.

A few days later I received an e-mail from Billy, asking if I'd like to do a bit of extra training to toughen up. We met twice: on the first occasion we swam in the cold waters of the Cam, and on the second we went running in the woods, where Billy rolled about in the mud and said he was becoming one with nature. Afterwards he pulled a thermos out of his rucksack with his filthy hands and we drank milky tea. I noticed him watching me out of the corner of his eye. Billy talked for a while about the smell of wet earth, then said he always felt so lonely among the boxers. I stood beside him and said nothing. I'd never spoken about how lonely I felt. Billy raised his plastic teacup to me. I offered him my hand; a bit formal, perhaps, but it felt right. The mud was sticky between our palms, and I think we both felt better together instead of alone.

*   *   *

The Pitt Club bar was so clean it shone. A bald waiter placed two glasses of a pink liquid we hadn't ordered on the counter. "Pitt Juice," said Billy, and knocked it back. I took a swig; the liquid tasted of vodka and lemonade. Billy leaned his back against the counter and stared at three very loud men for several minutes without speaking. The men all had the wiry, powerful bodies of trained boxers and wore light blue blazers with a red lion embroidered on the breast pocket. Without looking at me, Billy remarked that this was the blue blazer you got when you won a match against Oxford.

"Rich twats."

He reached for another glass.

"And the rest of the uni are on the outside dying to belong. There are only two sorts of people at Cambridge. Half of them are absurdly rich; the other half are trying to seem richer than they are. Sometimes I think I'm the only normal person here," he said.

I recognized one of the men in the blue blazers from training. He was tall and thin with blond hair and looked a bit like a surfer.

"Who's the surfer?" I asked.

"The tall guy? Never in a million years would he go surfing."

I nodded.

"The worst snob I've ever met. His name's Josh."

"Josh what?"

"Josh fucking Hartley."

"Not a friend of yours?"

Billy laughed and took a large swig of his drink.

"There's a story everyone here knows about that retard. One time he was out in London with a couple of friends, from Harrow, I think, having afternoon tea at the Goring."

"Where?"

"The Goring. Mega-expensive hotel. For fifty-five pounds you get as many scones and cucumber sandwiches as you like. For two hundred pounds you get as much Pol as you like to go with them."

"Pol?"

"Champagne, Hans. Pol Roger."

I felt my ears burn. I was the wrong man for this job. Billy bumped my forehead gently with his fist and carried on.

"It's good business for the Goring, actually, because the Asian tourists can only take half a glass of champagne and the Saudis don't drink alcohol but order the champagne anyway. Then along comes Hartley. He orders several bottles straight off the bat. The waiter hesitates, so Hartley takes a wad of twenty-pound notes and stuffs them in the breast pocket of his jacket. By the end of the evening the lads have secretly poured a couple of bottles of Pol into a vase of sunflowers. When the waiter brings the bill, Josh walks over to the dessert trolley. There's this couple sitting there, celebrating their tenth wedding anniversary. Hartley undoes his fly, plonks his dick onto an opera cake with white chocolate icing and says, 'I'd like to pay now.'"

"Oh," I said.

Billy didn't laugh. He shook his head slowly.

"He has a massive dick, apparently."

"How do you know all this?" I asked.

"No idea. Everyone knows that story."

"Huh."

"There's another one. His father has a Wikipedia entry where it says that he owns a castle and allegedly supports a successor organization of the fucking Blackshirts."

"Have you Googled him?"

Billy looked as if he were embarrassed by the question. I didn't know who the Blackshirts were.

The DJ turned the music up, and the bass thumped through the building with such force that dust trickled from the cracks in the paneled ceiling. The door opened and the first women entered the Club. The theme on the invitation had been "God." Three blonde girls had rolled themselves in gold dust and fastened angel wings to their backs. Another woman was wearing a robe of white, semi-transparent silk and had flowers in her hair. She walked up to me.

"Hi," she said.

"Hello."

"Do we know each other?" asked Billy.

She ignored him. "How do you like my costume?" said the woman, moving closer.

"Er, it's nice."

She tapped her chin with a finger.

"I'm a nymph." Her pupils were the size of gobstoppers. "Who's that?" she asked, pointing her thumb at Billy.

"That's—"

"I'm the opposite of a nymph," said Billy.

"Are you a member?" she asked me, paying Billy no further attention.

I shook my head.

"What's that necklace?" she asked.

Her fingers reached for the red gold chain around my neck; it had pushed up from underneath my collar.

"A present," I said. I regretted not having taken the chain off long ago.

An hour later the Club was so full I had to push people aside if I wanted to move. There were three times as many women as men. An angel and an Indian elephant god grabbed my hands and pulled me onto the dance floor.

The angel said, "The pre-party is usually better than the party, anyway."

I have never understood dancing. I didn't know what I was meant to do with my arms, but the dance floor was so full I could simply move with the crowd. A young woman accidentally elbowed me in the temple; another yelled something in my ear. One of them greeted me with a Nazi salute. Someone smelled of fried fish.

* * *

At boarding school I'd never gone along at weekends when the other boys took the bus to the disco two villages away. They would say they were going to a club, too, but they'd meant something different from this.

"Great party," one of the women yelled.

"Yes," I yelled back.

"The remix. Sick!" the woman shouted.

"Sick!" I shouted.

She took a little bag of pink pills out of her pocket and waved it before my eyes. The pills were stamped with the symbol for infinity.

"Already taken one," I yelled.

"Don't I know you from my Feuerbach lecture?" she yelled.

Two men carried a dwarf into the room on their shoulders. I looked into his eyes and saw nothing there. At some point the men started carrying the dwarf across the dance floor on their outstretched arms. Every now and then they dropped him. I saw condensed sweat dripping from the ceiling. One man held a bottle of Absolut to several girls' lips; they all drank, looking him in the eyes as they did so. The music was too loud. Someone tugged at my sleeve, and I jumped.

"Billy's getting beaten up," a young woman yelled.

I followed her into the inner courtyard. A group of men were standing in a circle. In the middle I saw Billy, so drunk he could hardly stand, and a tall, powerfully built man in a light blue blazer. I thought of my father and pushed my way into the circle.

"Get out of the ring, mate," said the man.

"Hans," said Billy. His nose was bleeding; the skin above his eye was split.

I raised my fists. The vodka was throbbing in my head. I was glad to be off the dance floor. The man threw a left hook without warning.

Long before that evening, in my first boxing lessons, I'd learned that it's not the punch that hurts, because skulls are hard; it's the humiliation. And because I was a small man who no one would expect to beat a hundred-kilo hulk in a light blue blazer, I could only win. You can't box well if you're afraid.

All evening I'd been playing a part. I'd behaved as if I thought it was normal for young men to wear light blue blazers and for women to roll themselves in gold dust. Ever since I'd arrived in Cambridge I'd thought every day about this club, and now I was standing in its backyard. I'd thought about what Alex could have meant when she said I had to solve a crime here. She'd cast me in a role to which I wasn't suited: I was supposed to play some kind of spy and to act brave, but I wasn't good at pretending to be someone I wasn't, nor had I had much opportunity so far to test my courage. In fact, I was sure I was a coward. And because this all made me nervous, I was glad when I finally found myself standing in front of a man who wanted to hit me. This was my moment: all the members of the Club were there.

Weeks later someone told me I'd looked as if I was dancing.

I didn't hit back. I slipped under the man's arm and put him in a lock. His breath turned my stomach. The man flung me away and dropped his fists.

"What's your name?" he asked.

"Hans."

"If I see your faggot friend here one more time, I'm going to smash his face in. Do you understand?"

Two minutes later the backyard was empty. Billy sank down on one knee and watched the blood from his nose pooling at his feet.

"Please . . . hospital," he said.

The nurse asked for the name of a relative who could be contacted if Billy's condition got any worse. Without looking up, Billy pointed at me. I gave the nurse my German ID card so she could write down my details. It had my real surname on it. I was probably the worst undercover investigator ever to attempt to solve a crime. I hoped Billy hadn't seen the name on the card, and promised myself I'd be more careful in future.

A doctor sewed up the cut on Billy's face. He said his nose wasn't broken, and that he had a blood alcohol concentration of 0.21.

The dwarf from the Pitt Club limped past the room where Billy was being treated. He glanced at me. His right arm was in a sling.

"They were playing bowls with me by the end," he said.

He reached into his jacket pocket, took out a crumpled business card and handed it to me.

"In case you ever have another party. There are a lot of fucking dwarves out there."

He raised his undamaged arm in farewell. I felt ashamed.

I helped Billy to the taxi, rode with him to his college, and sat beside his bed. The doctor had said he was so drunk there was a danger he might suffocate on his own blood. "Thanks," Billy said, before he fell asleep. He squinted at me through his swollen eyelids and added something I didn't quite understand. I thought I heard him say the word "truth."

The sun rose over the crenellated roofs of the college, and I stared into the light. I took my student ID out of my jacket pocket. It had my photo on it, *University of Cambridge* written across the top, and beside the photo: *Hans Stichler*, my new name.

Josh

It doesn't matter what you do if the stories they tell about you are good enough. The Goring story was strong. I suppose I should have felt a bit sorry for the waiter, because we're supposed to be polite to strangers, too. But you know what—fuck it.

Of course, there are some stories only a few people know, so only a few people can tell them. Often they're the best.

Another good story is that I would always get someone to give me an infusion to cancel out my hangovers. And of course I would always drink half a liter of coconut water the morning after a party, for the minerals and trace elements, though actually everyone did that at uni unless they were a total retard.

At midday I was staring at the needle in my arm and the tube attached to it. I watched the electrolyte solution entering me drop by drop, imagined it mingling with my blood and absorbing the alcohol. Whenever I was attached to a needle like this, I always felt the urge to jerk my arm really quickly and see if the needle would come out the other side below the elbow.

The previous night, after Paul fucked up the faggot—mate! All that blood!—he suggested we each drink at least one bottle of gin. Boom. Safe idea.

The medical student holding the electrolyte solution over my arm was in love with me and knew she could lose her university place for this. She was all right. She didn't have to do it; and whenever she asked me something, she really seemed to want to know what I had to say. I was still debating whether or not to shag her. When she looked down on me like that from above she always looked a bit like Sasha Grey.

"When are you going to take me to your castle?" she asked.

"Weather's not good right now."

These birds always want to go to the castle.

We haven't lived at Pengannon Castle for two generations. I grew up in a house on a cliff in Cornwall. It's painted Farrow & Ball Wimborne White. Sea view, long flight of steps up to the entrance. I'd trained there like a psycho all summer. By the end the veins were standing out on my forearms, pulsing against the skin. I'd come back from vacation weighing seventy-six kilos. Other boxers had got fat; after half an hour's warm-up some of them were jumping up and down in a puddle of their own sweat.

That summer I went running for an hour along the cliffs every morning. Afterwards I would drink a glass of coconut water and swallow six tablets of wild-harvested AFA algae, the original from Lake Klamath, to maintain an optimum balance of vitamin B12. I would breakfast on a bowl of chia seeds I'd left to soak the previous evening—very healthy because of the Omega-3 fatty acids. Then I would sit by my grandmother's bed and read her "The Devil's Sooty Brother." My grandmother is eighty-eight years old and has dementia, poor thing. Dementia is a bastard disease. I felt sorry for Grandma, I felt sorry for my mother, I even felt sorry for my father; it was so bad that all of us were thinking, *Hopefully Grandma will die soon.* Well, almost all of us. I don't think Grandma was thinking that; her brain was too far gone.

Sometimes, when I paused, Grandma would seize my hand and say, "Please, Daddy, just one more story, I'd like to hear 'The Devil's Sooty Brother,' too." She actually called me Daddy. She just wanted me to read her this one fairy tale over and over again.

I would often cry a bit before lunch (usually steamed salmon with broccoli—something low carb, anyway), but of course I knew it was my duty to read to my Grandma, because interpersonal relationships are the most important thing in life.

After lunch I would go to the gym in the nearest town and punch the sandbag. That summer I mainly worked on my left hook. I wasn't talented, but I knew that even without talent you could still be a boxer.

I kissed the student who was in love with me on the forehead and gave the warm fabric between her legs a quick stroke, but I still had too much alcohol in my system to get properly horny, so I gave her forty pounds to buy more electrolytes and left it at that. People always get this weird look in their eyes when you give them money; it's like throwing corn to chickens. Not that I've ever done that, of course—the chicken thing—but, you know, theoretically.

Then I went to the gym to flush the gin from my pores. Thought about friendship en route. A few days earlier I'd had to fill out an employee questionnaire for a bank where I was going to do an internship. The questionnaire had a field where you were supposed to write the name of someone to be contacted in case of emergency. I spent a long time thinking about who to put down. I didn't want to put my father, because I hardly knew him and didn't feel he deserved it. To put it bluntly, my father was an arsehole. I thought about all the lads I partied and trained with, but I didn't know whether any of them would describe me as his best friend. Isn't that what life is all about? Being able to call someone your best friend? A mate. Basically, I was living proof that money, a place at Cambridge, and a big dick don't make you happy. Fuck.

I'd seen the new German guy jumping rope at the other end of the boxing hall. He'd moved well yesterday evening, and now he was skipping quickly and easily, like a man who knows what he's doing—not exactly the norm at this retarded university. He was either very hard or very stupid.

I sensed that twinge in my scalp, a slight, pleasant pain spreading upward from the nape of my neck. I often felt it when something good was about to happen. This was one of the stories nobody knew; perhaps that was why it was strong. I'd felt it at the Goring. I'd felt it as a child when my father used to come home and bring me Turkish delight, but he didn't do that anymore.

Once, when I was a child, I'd found a cat in a dustbin on the street and brought it home. It was a tabby, and it was missing an ear. I know, it sounds wet, but she was lovely and soft. I hid her from my parents, asked our chauffeur if I could hide her in the garage and keep her; I gave her cream to drink, poured milk into my palm; I liked the roughness of her tongue. Once, just for a second, I held that little tongue between my index finger and thumb.

Three weeks later the cat was writhing on her blanket and I thought she was done for, rat poison or something, so I was very surprised when she squeezed out a litter. I watched this very closely. The chauffeur pointed at the kittens and told me I had to get rid of them.

I felt the same twinge that evening in the gym when I saw the German with the skipping rope, and silently hoped: Perhaps I've finally found somebody else like me.

Hans

The woman who was supposed to be helping me was sitting on the stairs outside my room when I came back from training on Saturday, the morning after the party. My vest was saturated with blood.

"What the hell happened to you, laddie?" she asked.

I couldn't help smiling. Blood always looked worse than it was. She'd even gone a bit pale.

"Your chin," she said.

"My chin?"

"It's covered in blood."

I wiped my face with the palms of my hands and felt the crustiness of dried blood.

"It's fine. Nothing broken. The other guy was just a bit better than me."

"I'd like to go to London with you. We need to go shopping," she said.

"Now?"

"Yes. And you should meet my father. He boxed for the university, too."

"OK."

"Do you have a dinner jacket?"

I sat beside her on the train with my dinner jacket in a suit bag on my lap. She took me to an antiques shop she said she used to go to with her father.

"One of these old suitcases was Hemingway's when he was out hunting lions in Africa," she said.

"Wow," I said, and hoped I sounded convincing.

The salesman greeted her with a kiss on the cheek and nodded at me. I noticed him looking at my jeans. On the train the young woman had said it was important I didn't look like new money.

She chatted to the salesman and walked around the shop as if it belonged to her. I stood in front of a root wood wardrobe, stared at the inlay and hoped this would soon be over. She bought a hard bag of untreated cowhide with a gleaming brown handle.

"For your boxing gear."

The bag was too small to hold my gloves, boxing shoes, protective cup and headguard, but I could see how pleased she was with the purchase.

"Thanks."

Afterwards we went to Camden Market and walked round the secondhand stalls. She bought me three pairs of shoes: one dark brown, one cognac-colored with little holes on the toe, and some black evening shoes. I didn't say much; I wondered when she would finally tell me her name. She took me to a sandwich shop where the sandwiches were like works of art. I ordered a cheese sandwich and the tattooed man behind the counter asked if I wanted Cabrales or Coulommiers. I was embarrassed; yet again I didn't understand. The strange young woman from Cambridge was standing beside me with the leather bag in her hand.

"Blue cheese or soft cheese?" asked the salesman.

"Soft."

She leaned over and spoke quietly in my ear: "I didn't know what the guy was talking about, either."

We both smiled, and sat down opposite each other, chewing.

"Charlotte," she said, and held out her hand. I wiped the mayonnaise off my forefinger.

"Hans."

"It's from riding," she said, pinching her shoulder muscles.

"What?"

"I'm an equestrian, so I do weight training. That's why my shoulders look the way they do."

For a moment I thought I saw her smile. Her hand was sticky.

"Thank you for paying for all this," I said.

She laughed as if I was joking.

We took the Underground to Sloane Square and walked from there to Charlotte's house. It was too big.

"I'm glad we have servants," she said, before we went in. "Otherwise I'd feel lonely here when I come to visit my father."

"You have servants?"

She laughed. "Embarrassing, isn't it?" Charlotte shifted from foot to foot. "What's your home like?" she asked.

"I don't have a home."

"Where did you grow up, then?"

"I haven't been back there for a long time. A house in the forest. I miss it. Smaller than this."

Neither of us knew what to say. Charlotte saved the moment before it got even more embarrassing.

"When Joyce, our cook, was a child in Jamaica, she learned how to make a superb Yorkshire pudding from English farmers on a sugarcane plantation."

"You have a cook from Jamaica?"

"Sometimes, when I come home, she sings Harry Belafonte."

A woman opened the door, smiling broadly.

"She's seen us," Charlotte said.

Joyce gave Charlotte a hug. She smelled of nutmeg. She nodded at me and said something in a strong accent, then went back into the kitchen, turning at the door and twinkling at Charlotte. We heard her singing quietly, a song about a little girl in Kingston town.

Charlotte took me up to the attic and opened a trunk full of shirts. She rummaged around in it, messing it up.

"My father put these aside to wear when he does the gardening."

"I see."

"He never does any gardening."

The shirts had been tailor-made for her father and had the initials *AF* on the left cuff. She handed me one.

"Put it on."

"Here?"

"Are you embarrassed to do it in front of me?"

As I took off my T-shirt I noticed Charlotte looking at my stomach muscles.

"Get the tailor to cut out the monogram," she said. She took a pile of shirts and gave them to me. "Father won't notice."

She paused for a moment and took my free hand. It was an intimate gesture, and I didn't know whether to return the pressure of her fingers.

"Listen, Hans. My father is a member of the Pitt Club. If he nominates you, you're in. Please can you talk a bit more this evening, not just say 'yes' and 'thanks'?"

"Yes," I said.

"Are you winding me up?"

She didn't let go of my hand, nor I hers. I spoke quietly, looking past her.

"But I don't know your father. What is all this?"

"You'll find out."

"I mean, what's so important that I have to lie to your father?"

She squeezed my hand.

"It is important. Just believe me."

"Charlotte, I—" I said, but she turned and dragged me across the attic. It was only at the top of the staircase that she let go of my hand.

Charlotte

Once a week I met up with a Chinese student and lied to him. We were doing a language exchange, talking about our daily lives, half an hour in English and half an hour in Chinese. The Chinese man called himself Peter because he said his real name was too complicated.

I didn't understand much when he spoke Chinese, though I didn't admit that to him. Then he would start speaking English, and it was perfect. He stressed every syllable, like a butler in the royal household.

Peter liked to talk about himself. He told me his father owned a company that manufactured controller chips for airplanes and medium-range ballistic missiles. He was an only child, a triathlete, and when he finished school he'd had to decide between Harvard, Yale, and Cambridge—he was accepted by all the universities he applied to. He said the president of Harvard had sent him a handwritten letter begging him to accept a place. He'd had the best exam results in the whole of northern China. Newspapers had written about him. He'd come to England because he liked rugby and orange marmalade, and he'd wanted to go to the Summer Olympics. When he said this he laughed, snorting as he breathed in. He also liked big-game hunting. Whenever we met, Peter was always wearing a light-blue bow tie.

At our first meeting he had asked what *branche* my father was in. He said *"branche,"* not "line of business," as if he were French. *I bet he speaks fluent French*, I thought. I looked out of the window, saw a woman in a fur coat and said that my father owned a coypu farm. I told him I'd gone to school in a village in Cumbria and that I'd had to help out on the farm in the afternoons, cleaning cages and skinning the coypu.

"Furs have to come from somewhere," said Peter.

It would only have taken him a few seconds to Google me and he would have seen where I actually went to school, and that a coypu farmer could not have paid the school fees. However, I trusted that I wasn't interesting enough to Peter for him to think of doing that.

One day, at the start of term, we met at Fitzbillies café. I drank water; Peter ate a cinnamon roll. The syrup ran down his chin and dripped onto his collar.

"I'd like to talk about the university clubs, Charlotte. I mean, we don't have things like this in China."

I could feel myself going red. "I don't know anything about that."

I stared at the syrup on his collar. He chewed quickly, dabbing at his upper lip with his napkin.

"Oh, I know quite a lot. In any case, there's only one name you need to know, Charlotte: the Pitt Club."

"Oh yes?"

"I'm becoming a member soon."

I reckoned he was lying; I couldn't see the Pitt Club admitting a guy from China.

"How do you become a member?" I asked.

He gave a tight smile.

"You know, Charlotte, it's the kind of club where you don't *ask* how to become a member," he said. "I mean, you're either one of them or you're not."

"And you're one of them?"

"It doesn't admit women, Charlotte."

"What a pity."

Fury rose up inside me. I think he noticed the change in my voice.

"I mean . . ."

"Do you know what they do in those clubs?"

"Well, they party, drink, have a good time, things like that."

Things like that. I thought about it every single day. Why me? That was the question I kept coming back to. Why me? But the question that kept me awake at night was: Why at all?

"You have no idea," I said.

"Charlotte, I—"

"Clubs like that are the lowest of the low. Misogynistic, elitist, stupid."

Peter was still smiling.

"Charlotte, I'm sorry I started talking about this, but I prefer to see for myself before making a judgment."

"Why are you all so obsessed with this club?"

Peter plucked at his bow tie.

"Why don't you go to one of their parties first, before you start criticizing it left, right, and center?"

I stood up, almost knocking my chair over, and headed for the door. Halfway there I turned, went back to the table, bent over Peter and said, as quietly as I could just then, "You sad fuck."

Outside in the fresh air, I wondered whether he'd deserved such an outburst. A few steps later I was quite sure that he had.

Hans

A servant had taken my shopping bags up to one of the guest rooms on the first floor. My dinner jacket was hanging on the clothes rail. This day was totally surreal. I turned the tap to cold and took a long shower, letting the water cascade onto my head. Charlotte had said I should come to her as soon as I was ready; she would be waiting for me. I'd stared at my feet and she had laughed.

I dressed and went up to the second floor. Her door was open. Charlotte was lying on her stomach asleep on the bed. She was wearing a high-necked black dress and no shoes and breathing deeply. Her blonde hair fell across her face; the dress was stretched tight across her shoulders. She looked as if her body temperature was always one or two degrees higher than other people's. Now, in sleep, she looked happy.

For some reason I still haven't fathomed, women like me. I realized it early on and wondered what it was they saw in me. I didn't know how to respond. It was strange; it didn't make sense that boys bullied me but girls liked me. And when the boys noticed it, they bullied me even more.

When I reached puberty a new interest in women awoke in me, one that initially took me by surprise, as it probably does most boys. I liked looking at girls, but even more than that I liked to smell them; they smelled of hay and vanilla ice cream, and something still unfamiliar to me. I could never have summoned the courage to approach a girl or a woman, but fortunately I never had to, and that was possibly the biggest puzzle of all for me.

In my village there were girls everywhere: at school, at the ice-cream parlour, in the hayloft in the new barn behind the football pitch. At boarding school I was surprised I met any women at all, because it wasn't that easy when you lived only with boys and monks; but I did meet them—when I went for walks in the forest, or on trips to Munich at weekends. One woman I slept with I met buying pretzels at the baker's.

Another woman, who already had children, sat next to me in a café in Munich one Sunday. Later, after we'd had sex, she smoked a cigarette on her balcony and told me I was the perfect man for an affair: quiet, with coal-black hair. At the time I felt very proud, because I was seventeen years old and she was already an adult; but then she said she could never marry a man like me, and asked me to leave because her husband and children would soon be back from the zoo. I didn't know what I was doing wrong. No woman ever said "I love you." I slept with women and I liked to breathe in the scent of their hair afterwards. The women were all so different, each one good in her own way. One of them told me she liked me because I was a serious lover.

When I was still very young I had asked my mother how I would know whether or not I loved someone, and she had said that when it happened, I would know.

A few years later a circus came to the village and pitched its tent beside a cornfield. The circus was called Kókoro. When I'd heard about it I'd run to the cornfield and asked if I could feed the big cats if I helped erect the tent. My main interests back then, depending on my mood, were big cats and breasts. Looking back now, I think there's no better time in life than these last days of childhood.

In one of the cages was a white tiger that had been de-clawed. I threw a beef shank through the bars, but the tiger ignored it. A few minutes later a girl with dark eyes and pale brown skin emerged from a caravan; she opened the cage door and went in, took the bone, and held it up in front of the tiger's nose. He ate out of her hands. The girl was perhaps three years older than me; she had small breasts and a flat, hard belly, though I didn't know that yet. She came out of the cage, took my hand and pushed it down the front of her trousers. I felt hair, and I liked it. She laughed, showing her white teeth, pulled my hand out of her trousers, encircled it with her fingers and didn't let go till we were deep in the cornfield. Her shirt was too short. On her back, just above her sacrum, were downy sun-blonde hairs I would have liked to touch. As she undressed me I stared at the dried blood on her fingers from the cow bone, too excited to be disgusted by it. She spoke to me in a foreign language. She was like me. Or so I thought, at fourteen years old.

I met her every day for the next two weeks. On the last day I wanted to ask her if she would stay with me; I knew

I would lose her if she moved on. For me she was the only woman I could love, besides my mother.

She left without saying goodbye. I didn't have a chance to ask her. Sometimes I fear she may never have existed at all.

I didn't know how I should wake Charlotte, because I didn't want to say the wrong thing; all day I'd had the feeling she was on the verge of shattering to pieces. I said her name but she slept on. I thought about slamming the door, but that seemed rude, and I was afraid one of the servants might see me in her room and misconstrue things. So I took the arch of her foot in my hand. It was very soft. Charlotte woke with a start; she leapt up and lashed out in my direction.

"Don't touch me!"

"I'm sorry."

She looked up at me. Her eyes were still sleepy; everything about her was warm. I wanted to tell her how beautiful she was just then.

"Charlotte . . ."

"Do you have another bow tie?" she asked.

I put my hand to my collar and didn't finish my sentence. She said that my tie was pre-tied and I needed a proper one. She'd be right back, I should hold on.

I had no idea what she was talking about.

A few minutes later she walked through the door, barefoot, and smiled at me. She had a black, untied, ribbed silk bow tie in her hand.

"I'll tie it for you," she said.

I sat down on a chair in front of the mirror, which extended from floor to ceiling. She tied the bow with slow movements, and although she tried to look as if she'd done it many times before, I noticed the little vertical line between her brows. I could smell the perfume she had sprayed on her wrists: orange peel and lily of the valley. Her little finger brushed my neck.

"It's my father's. He won't notice," she said.

We walked down the stairs. A man who could only be her father was standing on the marble floor at the bottom; he had hair like Charlotte's, just as thick and long but silvery blond, slicked down and combed back, the ends just touching his silk lapel. He kissed his daughter on both cheeks and looked at me. He was as tall as I was and must have been at least sixty, but he had the body of a young man: slender, athletic, full of energy.

"I want to know everything about the new boxing team. Angus Farewell."

His handshake was dry and firm.

"Hans Stichler," I said, and realized that I couldn't tear my eyes from his face. This man made me feel as if I were being received by a king.

The first course was tomato consommé, and with every spoonful I wondered how it was possible that something so colorless could taste so strongly of tomato. We sat at a too-large table in a room with curtains of pink raw silk. Everything looked expensive. The head of an exotic-looking bull hung on the wall. When Angus Farewell noticed me looking at it he said it was a Cape buffalo that he'd shot himself. The rifle, he said, was actually more beautiful than the buffalo, but he'd thought it would be silly to hang a gun on the wall. It was a .700 caliber falling-block rifle made by an Austrian gunsmith. I nodded. You handloaded it with a single bullet, he said. I looked at the buffalo's curved, projecting horns and wondered why some people felt the need to kill such a creature and hang its head in their living room.

"The gun's in the corner," said Farewell, "in case of intruders."

I looked at the corner.

"Behind the curtain," said Farewell.

Bread was served by a man in a dinner jacket who didn't introduce himself. I felt as if I were sitting in a restaurant, and listened as Charlotte chatted with her father. They talked about her PhD, her horse, and the upcoming race against Oxford. A large part of the conversation was about things I didn't understand, so I concluded that it was smarter to keep quiet. Charlotte looked at me and I knew I would have to say something soon, but I didn't know what, and the longer the two of them went on talking while I sat silently beside them, the more keenly I felt that I was failing whatever test this was.

Angus Farewell reached into his jacket pocket and pulled out a mobile phone. "Jesus Christ," he said, took the call, and left the room.

Charlotte got up and walked around the table. The look in her eyes made me briefly catch my breath. She stood behind me, placed one hand on the back of my neck, leaned forward and spoke quietly in my ear.

"Right, laddie, you just listen to me. I don't know where Alex dug you up, but you are going to pull yourself together and tell my father something about the bloody boxing team. You're boring him to death. You won't get anywhere like this."

Eyes closed, I breathed in her scent. All this time she had been gentle; now there was a hardness in her voice that surprised me.

Farewell's leather soles echoed down the corridor. Just before he came back into the room, Charlotte clouted the back of my head.

"Sydney," said Farewell, as if that explained something. He sighed, replaced his napkin on his thighs and stared at me, frowning.

"You all right there, my friend?" he asked.

Charlotte looked at me and gave a little scream. I glanced down and saw the blood that was dripping from my nose into the béarnaise sauce, streaking it red. The wound in my nose must have opened up again when Charlotte hit me on the head.

"It's from sparring. Please, forgive me." I had to smile; it was too stupid.

Farewell slapped the table. He looked delighted. Laughter lines creased his face.

"Welterweight, eh, Hans? May I call you Hans?"

"Yes. Welterweight." I looked down at the plate. "For now."

Charlotte laughed. I was a little puzzled: I couldn't remember the last time I'd tried to be funny.

"Please may I get some ice from the kitchen? I don't want to ruin your tablecloth."

"Of course—wait, I'll go down with you. I know what it's like; some chap from Oxford smashed my nose once. I bled like a geyser."

He got up and went with me to the kitchen.

The rest of the evening the conversation was all about boxing. Charlotte leaned back in her chair, smiling quietly at me. When her father stood up during the *mousse au chocolat* to demonstrate a combination that had won him one of his fights, Charlotte raised her glass and nodded at me.

After the meal she said she was tired and wished us goodnight. She hugged her father and kissed me on the cheek, putting her hand on the back of my neck as she did so.

Angus Farewell said he wanted to show me something. He handed me two heavy tumblers and went down a staircase to the cellar. Part of the cellar was filled to the ceiling with wine bottles; there was also a shelf of whisky.

"Do you know anything about whisky?" asked Farewell.

"Absolutely nothing." Wine had made me brave.

"Nor did I at your age."

He took a bottle from the shelf and we walked through the cellar. He pressed a series of switches. Neon lights illuminated a boxing ring; beside it, two sandbags hung from the ceiling.

"My home," said Farewell. He unscrewed the bottle and filled the tumblers.

The whisky tasted of peat and caramel. Farewell said he hoped I would box against Oxford in the spring. Thirty-nine years ago he had won his weight category. It would be an honor to see me fight for Cambridge in the same weight class as him.

"What do you want to do with your life, Hans?" he asked.

We leaned back against the ropes and stared into the depths of the room, as if an answer were hidden there. For a moment I considered whether I ought to say something that sounded ambitious.

"No idea, to be honest."

He raised his glass and clinked it gently against mine.

"To freedom," he said, and drank.

I felt that I needed to say something else.

"I mean, I don't know what field I want to go into, but I would like to have a family one day. And do something that'll allow me to be myself."

"Who else could you be?"

I said nothing. Farewell put his hand on my shoulder and left it there.

"That sounds very sensible. See what happens at Cambridge; it'll all fall into place."

"What do you do, actually?" I asked. I couldn't bring myself to call him Angus.

"I'm an investment manager with an independent private equity company."

"Ah, right."

He laughed. "I work for a holding company that focuses on expansion and growth financing in the public health sector. So we buy up companies with other people's money, trim them for profitability, then sell them on a few years later to the next buyer."

"Aha."

"Which means I work for locusts," said Farewell, "and make sure a lot of money is turned into even more money, and between you and me it's an absolutely ridiculous profession. If ever you consider going into it yourself, I will forbid Charlotte to have anything to do with you."

I thought about how I had introduced myself with a false name, how Charlotte had only brought me to this house to get her father to nominate me at the Pitt Club. And I still didn't know what crimes were being committed there that were important enough for me to have to move from Germany to Cambridge, and Charlotte to have to deceive her own father.

After a while Farewell said he would have the car brought round; next time I should stay the night and we should spar a few rounds in the ring.

"Look after Charlotte," he said.

I nodded. I hardly felt nervous any more. "She seems so wounded," I said, hoping he wouldn't take it the wrong way. Farewell nodded.

"It's the place. Cambridge. I think for some it can be damaging."

"It's the people," I said.

"What do you mean?"

"The place is just a place. It's people who do damage."

He nodded again. "Look after Charlie," he said; then, very quietly: "Please."

Angus Farewell took a deep breath; when he spoke again his voice was firm. He bounced his torso once against the ropes.

"Because—you know."

"Yes, I know," I said, although I didn't understand a thing.

As the car drove towards Cambridge I stared out of the window at the night, exhausted and yet wide awake. The alcohol and the excitement were at odds with each other and were churning me up inside. The car was big and black; the chauffeur was silent. I didn't belong to these people, but there had been moments that evening when I'd felt that I could. I wanted to note down the name of the whisky, but I couldn't remember it. Perhaps the whisky itself was to blame, or perhaps it was because these past few days had all been a bit too much, but I wanted Angus Farewell to be my friend. His laughter lines reminded me of my father; it was just a trick of nature, but this detail made me feel warm towards him. I'd enjoyed talking to him about the team, and I'd felt close to him when we'd stood in the cellar leaning against the ropes. The boxing cellar was amazing. I'd never seen anything like it. The ropes around the ring were black, the sandbags were leather, and on the wall, neatly lined up one after another, were glass cases with exotic butterflies in the most brilliant colors.

Josh

Searching for tomatoes in November was an absolutely re-tarded idea. I walked across the market square, stopped, looked at the beef tomatoes and sniffed them. I plucked a cherry tomato from its vine and ate it. No good; too late in the year.

I was going to cook that evening for the new German from the boxing club. As in: I was going to cook and he was going to eat. To be honest, this was my way of trying to please him. I liked him. Not in a gay way—as a friend.

I bought lamb's lettuce, oyster mushrooms and shallots, and chervil for the vinaigrette. I went to The Art of Meat and bought a thick piece of organic Hertfordshire beef fillet. I always bought organic meat. Intensive animal husbandry is immoral and disgusting, and people who support the industry are bastards. Oil's another one. Almost every single face cream is petroleum based. Petroleum!

The way the butcher introduced the knife into the flesh and cut along the bone . . . mate! I liked that knife.

At eight o'clock the doorbell rang. Stichler was holding a bottle of white wine; I could tell immediately that it was from the supermarket. He sat down on a stool beside the cooker. He was wearing a great shirt; it was pale blue and shimmery, expensive cotton, Giza perhaps, or Sea Island. A lot of people think it's all about the label; they run off to Armani and get themselves expensive shirts. When I was a child my father's tailor explained to me that it's actually all about the quality of the material and the handiwork. He didn't sew labels in his suits.

My kitchen was equipped with a gas cooker and a marble worktop. It was the best kitchen I'd managed to find in Cambridge. I'd had the walls painted this insane gray—Farrow & Ball Bone.

I plucked, washed, then spun the lamb's lettuce, chopped the shallots, sliced the mushrooms. I fried them in butter, which was a little tricky because I had to keep the temperature below the smoke point, but I mean: how sexy is butter?

The fillet of beef was sitting in a tin in the oven at 140 degrees Celsius. Meat tastes much more like meat without the roasted flavour, in my opinion. By cooking it in this way

I could reduce the amount of fat needed to an absolute minimum. When the core temperature reached 58 degrees Celsius, I took the meat out of the oven.

"You can really cook," said Stichler.

How many times had I heard this sentence? Hardly anyone at Cambridge could cook. The students were spoiled because they'd grown up in boarding schools. I had this French nanny once, the one with the peach. She's the one who taught me; but that's a different story.

I mixed a vinaigrette for the salad, stirred in the mushrooms and shallots, coated the meat with butter and sprinkled it with coarse sea salt and crushed peppercorns, cut the fillet into thick slices and dressed it. À la minute, motherfucker.

Then I told him. "I was at the Pitt Club yesterday, brother. Your name was in the book."

It was sick, saying this and watching the change in his expression. Stichler had this classical face and buff hair.

He gaped at me like a fish. He didn't say anything, so I just kept talking.

"Angus Farewell nominated you. I've seconded."

The meat was tender and flavorful; the salad tasted great, as well.

I liked this Hans Stichler more and more. A quiet customer, but a beast in the ring. Some days we shared a sandbag; neither of us would say much, but I could feel that we were building a connection. At least, I hoped so. Saying nothing is incredibly stylish, too. I've always thought that.

"Some more beef, Stichler?"

"It's delicious."

"Thanks."

"Do you have a bit of bread to go with it, perhaps?" he asked.

"You eat bread?"

Stichler looked at me, wide-eyed. "Don't you?"

"Have you ever considered how dangerous gluten is for your digestive system? All I'm saying is: wheat belly. Spelt's just about OK, but since everyone's started baking with genetically modified wheat I really would steer clear of it."

Mate—the look on his face! Stichler didn't respond, but we understood each other all the same.

Late that evening, after he'd left, I poured the rest of the cheap white wine down the drain, threw the shallot skins in the bin, put the dirty plates in the dishwasher, and wiped down the marble worktop. I drank another half bottle of champagne to clear my head. I came across the chervil in the brown paper bag from the market. I'd forgotten it. I stared into the bag and could feel the energy inside me getting too much; it had to come out. It had been a nice evening, and now I had to throw the chervil away because it would be withered by morning. I hated wasting things.

Marble is a hard surface. Any child knows that.

I picked up the stool Stichler had sat on by the legs and slammed it down on the marble worktop, again and again, until the wood splintered into pieces.

Hans

As I walked down Castle Street I felt the cotton against my skin and saw the spot on the left cuff where the tailor had removed the initials.

I passed my college and turned into Jesus Lane. The Pitt Club stood white and glowing in the night. Six Ionian columns supported the roof outside the entrance to the clubhouse. I placed my hand on one of the cold pillars. The building looked like a temple, and more than ever I felt a desire to belong. For a moment I tried to convince myself that the desire had been awakened by Alex's mission, but I knew that it had in fact been growing in me for a very long time.

I had to go home and write an essay about Karl Marx; I was supposed to have finished it by the next morning. I liked the wording of the question: "'In direct contrast to German philosophy, which descends from heaven to earth, here we ascend to earth from heaven' (Marx). Discuss."

Angus

Chelsea: light-bathed windows, tall hedges, white gravel drives. It almost doesn't feel like London. I think that's why I've always liked it there.

Until I went to boarding school I lived in a manor house in Somerset. Silence at night, the smell of blossom in the morning, waiting for the day of the first cider pressing. That was my childhood.

There were times when the concrete and blinking lights of London depressed me. Underground trains are the great sin of civilization. You stand there penned in like a pig en route to the slaughterhouse, breathing in strangers' exhalations, it's too hot, and someone is always sneezing. The most vulgar form of transport imaginable. When I think of the faces of people emerging from the tunnels of the Underground it immediately puts me in a foul mood.

They say that Londoners are always nasty to strangers. I actually think Londoners are the friendliest of people until they get on the Underground every morning and lose their minds.

I hereby solemnly swear that if I should ever become poor and have only ten pounds in my pocket, I will spend those ten pounds on a taxi, just to avoid the Underground.

The house of the investment banker who had invited us that evening stood at the end of a long drive. White gravel, naturally. Lining the path to the house were large stone sculptures of butterflies. Jesus Christ. Two butlers were waiting on the threshold; they wore top hats and cream gloves. How can anyone make their butler wear a top hat in the twenty-first century? I couldn't suppress my laughter.

There were about forty men at the house. I knew them all. Close-shaved cheeks, thinning hair, the scent of forty aftershaves, all with a faint whiff of cedar.

A few of the younger ones were playing billiards in the basement; in the garden two men were sitting on a swing seat drinking Negronis, which a butler was carrying round the house on a silver tray. The host was the financial director of a private bank who for the past couple of years had been working one day a week in an honorary capacity as an advisor at Amnesty International's London headquarters. I was willing to bet he took the Underground when he went to Amnesty. He wore fat ties, smoked thin white cigarettes, drank white wine diluted with soda, and laughed too loudly. Nouveau riche in every fiber of his being. I thought it was a shame I'd never boxed against the man.

The host greeted me with a hug and said if I needed anything I should ask George.

"Which one is George?"

"I call them all George," said the host, "otherwise I get confused."

*   *   *

At the piano stood my saving grace in the form of Prince Amha Makonnen Workq. He was sporting a midnight-blue dinner jacket and eating a prawn canapé.

"Amha, you old bastard," I said.

"Farewell, what a pleasure to see you. Fancy a prawn?"

Forty years earlier the prince and I had both spent a season boxing for the university. He became a Butterfly the year after I did. He was the first colored man to be admitted to the Club. I remember the discussions at the time. The fact that he was a prince from the House of David worked in his favor. At university he wore a black velvet collar on all his suits to express his sorrow that his family had been driven out of his country by the coup. I also had a black velvet collar sewn on a tweed jacket, out of solidarity, and this cemented our friendship. To this day Amha and I still go to the same tailor, a man from Vienna who comes to London six times a year for fittings.

That evening we talked about our daughters. Peeling the prawn with manicured fingers, the prince said his daughter was a disaster academically, but would go up to Cambridge in two years' time. She also wanted to study art history, like Charlotte. Art was perfect for a princess, he said; that way she'd never get bored in the palace, it was full of pictures.

I remembered the prince telling me about his university interview. While other prospective students were busy writing essays and taking exams, he arranged to go for a stroll around the rose garden with the Master of the college. At the end of their stroll, the Master apparently said he was looking forward to having a student in college who was personally acquainted with most of the people after whom the roses in the garden were named.

"Tell me, have you heard these stories about the younger members?" I asked. The subject had been making me nervous ever since the Norwegian ambassador had told me over lunch a few weeks earlier that current members were spiking women's drinks with liquid ecstasy.

The prince popped another prawn into his mouth.

"Yes, but come on, relax. On another subject: Have you heard about this Japanese whisky? Two hundred pounds a bottle; they say it's as rounded as a billiard ball. I saw a bottle out front."

I wondered if I wanted to know what a billiard ball tasted like.

"I thought you'd had a stroke?"

"I'm a prince. I'm allowed to drink even though I've had a stroke."

I liked him because he didn't take himself as seriously as most of the other princes I knew. Prince Amha lived in a small house in North London with his wife, a doctor from Kent; he always had money problems, and knew for certain that he would never see the palace in his homeland again.

One of the Georges sounded a pair of cymbals. We entered the dining room. The people standing round the table were mostly bankers, but there were also two ambassadors, the Leader of the House of Lords, a prince, five dukes, the head of an auction house, the deputy head of MI6, the editor-in-chief of the *Spectator*, and me. I thought that if someone were to throw a grenade into this room right now, people would wake up tomorrow in a different country.

Beside me sat the prince, and a duke who was talking to the *Spectator* editor-in-chief about how the aristocracy never got the coverage to which it was entitled. It was inexpressibly boring. George carried in two roast pheasants, followed by another George with another two pheasants. The men ate the birds and talked about boxing and their mistresses. Laughter, South African red wine, flushed faces, brown sauce dripping onto starched shirts. I found myself thinking of Dante.

I didn't get drunk, although I did drink a lot. The party began to make me feel uneasy. Perhaps it had all been a mistake. Charlotte was of an age at which women got invitations from the Butterflies. Hopefully she was too smart to accept such an invitation.

I said goodbye to the prince, walked up the gravel drive to the street and paused in front of one of the stone butterflies. I had a bottle of the Japanese whisky in my hand; one for the road. I glanced around and kicked at the statue's wings. It was a powerful kick, and for a second I was proud of how strong I still was, with my sixty years; then my sole slipped on the mossy stone, I lost my balance and fell over on the damp, dewy grass. I lay there looking up at the sky, feeling like an idiot. I stayed there a while longer. It smelled almost like the Somerset apple orchards of my childhood. A few deep breaths, a hand on the grass, a moment of quiet. I drank a mouthful of the whisky lying down and poured the rest out onto the lawn.

Hans

Most of the boxers jogged together. "Attacking the road," my coach called it. Billy didn't jog because he had knee problems, or so he said. Everyone suspected that he was just too lazy. I liked to run in the evenings before I went to bed, through the meadows behind the city. I ran alone. Every time I ran past the paddock with Charlotte's horse I brought it an apple and enjoyed feeling close to it.

That night in November I was running across the meadows, thinking about the next fight, or about nothing at all. I didn't care whether or not my sweatshirt was clean, or if I looked ridiculous in my bobble hat; what mattered was that I was running as fast as I could. I'd thought a lot about what boxing training actually was. Training gave you the chance to accustom your body to pain. As a child I tried to avoid pain, punching less hard when the trainer wasn't looking. As a student, I went looking for pain. I think a boxer has to love the fight, not the victory. When I watched footballers training they would laugh and mess around. Nobody laughed in the gym of the Cambridge University Amateur Boxing Club.

I saw two people standing by the paddock fence, but I couldn't make out their faces in the dark, so I ran closer.

The two people by the paddock were Charlotte and a man. They were holding hands. It looked wrong somehow. I wanted to turn and run the other way.

"Hans."

Charlotte called to me. I was out of breath. She introduced the man, smiling as if she had understood nothing. "This is Magnus, my boyfriend," she said.

He was blond and looked as if he was probably good at golf. I wondered why he didn't have any stubble.

"Are you visiting?" I asked.

The blond man laughed. His teeth were white and even. He slapped me on the shoulder. My left hand twitched briefly; for a moment I saw panic in Charlotte's eyes, and I knew that she understood everything.

The blond man didn't notice. He laughed with his mouth wide open, as if I'd told a good joke.

"I'm doing my PhD in Economics, but I'm actually a consultant at BCG."

I didn't know what BCG was, nor did I care. Charlotte and the blond man made a couple of bland remarks. I thought of how her little finger had brushed my neck as she tied my bow tie.

"Nice to meet you," I said. "Excuse me—I'm training—got to go—good luck."

I turned and ran off into the night. Why had I said good luck? I ran faster, and forgot the blond man's face.

Peter

Alarm: 7 a.m.

Sport: 50 press-ups, dips, 2 planks 30 seconds each

Masturbation: during breakfast

Breakfast: instant noodles with *jiaozi*

Motto of the day: One can know how to win without being able to do it.

Aim of the day: Write to the African prince; be the best.

Dear Prince Makonnen Workq,

My name is Peter Wong and I am a student at Peterhouse College, Cambridge. You don't know me, but you and I have something in common. We both came to Cambridge as foreigners. You came shortly after the coup in your African homeland. I came because what I seek does not exist in my homeland, China. I came for the Pitt Club, because it is an institution that brings forth greatness. I would like to ask you, as an alumnus, to support my admittance to the Club. You were the first dark-skinned member; I would like to be the first member from China. I know that you are a member because I found an old photo of the Committee in the library in which you appear.

I am the son of Wong Bao Wen, the CEO of the Northern China Technology Corporation. I passed the Chinese national higher education entrance examination, the gaokao, as the best student in Beijing, and I run a marathon in 3 hours 17 minutes. I speak Mandarin, English, French, and a little Hakka. At Cambridge I gained a First in my Part One examinations. I am a member of the Union Society, the Athletic Club, the Wine and Cheese Appreciation Society, and the Croquet Society. I have many friends at the Pitt Club, but I think it would be helpful if you were to write my name in the book in the entrance hall.

I would like to express my gratitude by supporting your fight for justice in your homeland and would appreciate it if you could let me know how I might support your foundation, idealistically or financially. I would be happy to come to London to introduce myself in person.

I look forward to your reply.

Yours sincerely,

Peter Wong

Hans

Shortly before the end of term I was lying on the parquet floor of my room. I had strained my back that morning and couldn't sit or lie down without pain. It was more bearable if I lay on a hard surface and propped my feet up on the edge of the bed. I was reading a book about a book by Foucault.

I was naked; I always slept naked, even when it was cold.

There was a knock at the door. I pulled on a pair of jeans and went to open it. Angus Farewell was standing outside in a dinner jacket. He laughed in my face and tossed his long silver hair.

"Get dressed," he said. "We have an appointment."

I went back into my room, surprised by how pleased I was to see him. I splashed my face with cold water, put on a shirt and started to tie my new bow tie. I'd found it in my pigeonhole a few weeks ago, after the night by the paddock; it was in a brown paper envelope with no note, but I knew it had come from Charlotte. I'd practiced tying it for two weeks, a few minutes each day.

I was still tucking in my shirt when I stepped back into the corridor. Farewell was leaning against the wall, fine fabric on whitewashed plaster.

"Where are we going?" I asked.

He was walking downstairs ahead of me, and I couldn't see his face.

"To the Pitt Club. The Committee has decided to admit you," he said.

I followed him, speechless. Every stair brought me a step closer to my goal, but with every step I was betraying the man who had lent me his support.

I stopped at the bottom and held out my hand. Everything about this felt wrong.

"Thank you, Mr. Farewell," I said.

"Please—call me Angus."

We walked to the Pitt Club in silence. A clammy chill had risen from the river and descended on the town. Neither of us was wearing a coat, but I was too nervous to feel the cold. We entered the Club and went upstairs. Before me stood at least thirty men in a row, all in evening wear. Around their necks they wore the Pitt Club bow tie: silver, blue, and black stripes. Farewell and I walked towards the bar, and each of the men shook my hand. I wished I had a handshake like Farewell's, firm and dry; my palms were damp.

Two metal goblets stood on the counter, filled with champagne. Out of the corner of my eye I saw Farewell down his in one, and I emptied my goblet, too. He tugged at the end of my bow tie, loosened it, put it in my suit pocket, and tied a Pitt Club tie around my neck.

"To Hans Stichler," Farewell declared to the room. Then he leaned towards me and said, "You're one of us now." The men raised silver goblets and called out my false name, which they pronounced "Stickler." Nevertheless, I was proud.

The evening passed to the rhythm of popping corks. The lilies in the vase by the wall exuded a scent that gave me a headache. I wondered who was paying for the drinks. I saw the faces of men I knew from university; some of the boxers were there, too.

From time to time one of the older men came up to me and made small talk or asked me which college I was at.

"What's the totty like this year?" asked one.

"What does your father do?" asked another.

"Do you hunt?" asked the next, before launching into a long speech about the merits of the German dachshund.

Josh hugged me. I found the physical contact unpleasant. He apologized for forgetting to put chervil in the vinaigrette and said we had to thrash Oxford this year. He kept on gently slapping my face.

"Boom, boom, boom," he said.

I ran my hand along the wooden counter of the bar and placed my palm over a spot where the varnish had chipped off.

A hand grabbed me and pulled me to the door, down the stairs and outside, where cold air streamed into my lungs. It was Farewell.

"A little walk," he said.

I thought of my father's laughter lines. We walked to St. John's College; the porter let us through the gate without asking any questions, as if he knew Farewell. We sat on the wall of the bridge over the Cam.

I wanted to tell him about Alex but I didn't know how to start. She'd never been there for me, not until she needed me. I was lying for her, I hated it, and I didn't know how long I could keep it up.

"Hans?"

Farewell was looking at me. I'd been daydreaming.

"Are you looking after Charlotte?" he asked again.

"I thought the Swede was doing that?" I said. I was rather drunk.

"The Swede isn't one of us."

Farewell spat into the water.

"Never take her to the Club," he said.

I was silent.

"And you must come to London next week. My tailor is over from Vienna. You need a new dinner jacket."

I'd bought my dinner jacket for eighty-nine euros and ninety-nine cents before moving to England, from an online shop called Alibaba. The trousers sagged like a burst balloon. I'd thought no one would notice.

"I'd love to come, but I'm afraid I can't afford it."

"Don't worry about that."

He put an arm around me; as a father might embrace his son, I thought, but perhaps I was wrong.

I wasn't religious, but that night, as I entered my room and fell into bed fully clothed, I made an attempt at a prayer: "Dear God, thank you for letting me meet a man like Angus Farewell."

All my life I'd dreamed of having friends and belonging somewhere, and now the dream had come true because I was a fraud. Alex had told me I had to solve a crime in the Pitt Club. Some of the men at the Club had a strange way of talking about women; it sounded as if they despised them. Far stranger to me than these men were the women who knew what they were like yet still came to the parties. I couldn't imagine Farewell being part of anything where people were actually doing something wrong.

I had the sense that I hadn't told God enough.

"And . . . please show me the right thing to do."

I lay on the mattress and thought about the evening, which had been a good one, and about all the other evenings to come. I put one foot on the ground beside the bed to stop the world spinning quite so violently. My back pain was completely gone.

Josh

There are, of course, advantages and disadvantages to living a long way out of town. The big disadvantage is that it's a fucking long walk home.

I fell over a couple of times. I threw up in a bush in someone's front garden. Absolutely first-class puke; I'd hardly eaten anything because I had to keep my weight down, so the stream flowed smoothly from my throat.

I saw a terracotta garden gnome beside the bush and took it with me, singing a nursery rhyme I'd learned from my first nanny.

> Rond, rond, rond
> La queue d'un cochon.
> Ri, ri, ri
> La queue d'une souris.

I felt sick, but happy. I was pleased for Stichler; we would become friends now, I could feel the connection between us. I'd become really obsessed with the friendship thing. If I hadn't known better I'd have thought I was a faggot. I just wanted to spend time with him, chatting about this and that. I wanted him to be my mate.

I sat on a bench for a few minutes, singing. When I started to feel cold I walked on, thinking about gin and the next Varsity match. Just before I reached my flat I went into another front garden and undid my fly. I didn't see the bitch standing in the shadow of the doorway, smoking. My stream hit a rosebush; my dick was in my hand and I was thinking about how other men were good at math, playing the violin, or French. I'm good at shagging, I thought, and felt smug. When the bitch behind me started talking I was so startled that I lost my balance and fell into the rosebush.

"I hope that rose doesn't take after you or it'll always be tiny," she said.

Her voice was calm. I walked up to her; she looked me dead in the eye, which I thought was pretty rude. She had hair like a man's, close-cropped, a number two.

"Get the fuck off my property," she said.

She tried to turn away, but even after four bottles of champagne I was too quick for her. I got her with a left hook, with the palm of my hand. You don't hit women with a fist.

Boom.

The force of the blow knocked her over. I didn't say a word; I spat in her direction and walked off without looking back.

Ra, ra, ra
La queue d'un gros rat.

The terracotta gnome was cool in my hand. From now on he would sit on my windowsill beside the pots of basil and rosemary.

Peter

Alarm: 7 a.m.

Sport: 52 press-ups, 30 dips

Masturbation: after reading post, three times, to calm down

Breakfast: instant noodles with *jiaozi*

Motto of the day: If you're planning to do something, act as if you're not.

Aim of the day: Climb the spruce opposite the Pitt Club and keep watch; be the best.

Dear Mr. Wong,

Many thanks for your letter. Unfortunately I cannot see any way in which I might help you with your endeavours. I do not

maintain contact with any clubs connected to the University of
Cambridge.
    Sincerely yours,
    Amha Makonnen Workq

Alex

I bought the expandable baton on Amazon for fourteen
pounds through a friend's account and had it sent to her
post office box in London. It was sixty-three centimeters long,
with a rubberized handle and a steel ball on the tip. One of
the customers had left a review: *It is made of attractive, shiny*
metal and is very robust. When tested on a metal table the baton
did not sustain any damage. Very nice! I had never used such
an implement, but the customer review convinced me.

I found out where he lived the night he hit me, then went
home and washed my face. He didn't see me follow him.
    From then on, every evening, I put on black clothes,
slipped the baton up my sleeve and waited in a hedge outside
his house. I'd been waiting every night for two weeks. It was
cold, and the hedge was crawling with spiders. I knew he
would come, and I wanted to meet him at night, when the
road was dark and everyone was asleep. I had learned in the
past to be patient.

Standing there in the hedge I thought about Hans. Charlotte had told me how well he got on with her father. The boy was so lonely.

One night, a few weeks earlier, I'd seen him walking down Castle Street. It sounds crazy, but when I'd realized he wasn't going back to his room in College I followed him. He stepped softly, as if checking with each step that there was nothing in his path that he might crush by mistake. His mother used to walk the same way. I missed her. Back then, sitting at table with her and Hans in the house in the forest, I realized what it meant to be a family. We all held hands before dinner, and I felt safe.

When I saw Hans that evening in Cambridge, standing and staring at the white pillars outside the Pitt Club and looking lost, I had an overwhelming urge to go and hug him. I imagine being a mother must feel a bit like that. I stayed in the shadows.

Being a mother—how absurd that sounds. As if it were a profession. I'd never have thought I'd imagine I could understand what it was like. But then neither would I have thought that I would one day be almost sixty years old and spending my nights in a hedge waiting for a man.

When he came I pulled the balaclava over my face, took the baton from my sleeve, stepped silently out of the hedge and booted the backs of his knees. When he was on the ground I let the steel ball rain down. Twenty, maybe thirty blows to the torso. I was careful to aim well. A blow to the head could have split his skull, and things would have got too complicated. When I got tired I spat in his face. He had closed his eyes. How easy it was to get a man to close his eyes and stop moving.

At home I slid the baton under my mattress, took a hot shower, and moisturized my skin. Now it was just up to Hans to play his part. What a good thing it was that he had come. For the first time in years I slept without fully lowering the blind.

Hans

"You look terrible."

Alex was sitting bolt upright in her chair. I knew she was right. It was late February; the match against Oxford was in five weeks. I was eating nothing but steamed chicken breast and salad without dressing, as I still had to lose another four kilos to reach my weight category. I ate just once a day. My skin had taken on a sickly grayish sheen.

It was February; it was raining that day and had got dark early. A fire was burning in the grate. I had read in the rules that open fires were banned everywhere in College. I could see little holes in the ceiling of Alex's room where the smoke alarms must have been.

Alex wanted to discuss my progress, as she'd put it in her e-mail. I'd been at the university for five months and had realized it was a place that had a lot to offer. There were indeed some geniuses among the students, but the majority just worked really hard. Some of them would fall asleep over their books in the library; lots of students took Ritalin to cope with the pressure. There was a girl in my college who had a sound-proof room because she practiced the violin for eight hours every day. There was a supposedly nymphomaniac Philosophy student from Russia who knew more about Hegel than the lecturers, and a young man writing a PhD on mouse brains who snapped the necks of four mice a day, on average, so he could look inside their skulls. Most students knew that the Pitt Club existed, but they also knew that they weren't member material, so they didn't pay much attention to it, apart from talking occasionally at parties about the latest rumours concerning the Club and secretly hoping they would be invited there one day.

I enjoyed lectures, and I spent a lot of time studying in a side wing of the University Library devoted to Old Norse literature, somewhere I could be alone. It was the old part of the library that could only be accessed through a side door; there was no Wi-Fi, so most students didn't like to work there. It smelled of dust and old glue. I often had a feeling that the books had little messages from Charlotte in them. I trained every day and usually went to the Pitt Club twice a week for lunch, but that didn't make much sense during this period because the cook didn't do steamed chicken breast. I hadn't observed any crimes being committed at the Club. I told Alex all of this, and she listened.

She went over to a French window, opened it, and stepped onto the balcony. The wind blew into the room. Alex stood in the rain; she was wearing a short-sleeved shirt and jeans. I waited a moment, then threw on my coat and went to join her. There were no lampposts in Chapel Court; the only light came from windows where students sat at their desks, illuminated by their reading lamps. Alex asked if the cold bothered me.

I stood beside her, studying her thin face. In the last few months I'd kept hoping she would want to meet up, but my encounters with Alex were always brief; she remained distant, and it felt as if I were reporting to my boss.

A few weeks before this meeting I'd found an interview with her online, a scan of an old newspaper article. She was talking about having taken a year off to climb a few mountains; it had been the year after my mother died. That winter Alex had run a 430-kilometer race along the frozen bed of the Yukon River in Alaska. It was called the Yukon Arctic Ultra and was considered to be the toughest ultramarathon, with temperatures below minus fifty degrees Celsius. In the interview she talked about how her long johns had been too big, meaning that the seam cut into the muscle of her thigh. She couldn't take the underpants off because she'd have risked freezing to death. Alex ran all the way to the finish line, placing thirty-fourth out of hundreds of participants; all the runners who finished ahead of her were men. The doctors had cut off her long johns in a cabin. The flesh of her thigh had been abraded right down to the muscle.

"Why did you keep running back then, in Alaska?" I asked.

Alex wiped the rain from her nose. "Do you believe in ghosts?" she asked.

"What?"

"There are meant to be ghosts here in College. Haven't you heard? In Second Court. Supposedly it's the ghost of a former student, James Wood, who studied here a hundred and fifty years ago. He was so poor he couldn't afford to buy wood for a fire. He fell asleep over his books and froze to death, and his ghost has haunted students ever since."

"Why is it so hard to talk to you, Alex?"

"For a long time I didn't believe in ghost stories," she said.

"Why are you telling me this?"

"In the Yukon Delta I was running away from a ghost."

Alex was shivering. Her shirt was wet, and through the material I could see the straps of her black bra against her skin. I stepped back into the room; the situation was making me uncomfortable, and I stared at the gaps between the floorboards. Alex went into the little bathroom and came back in a gray pullover and leggings. She said she was pleased with me, and to carry on just as I was. She talked to me as if I were one of her students who had written a good essay.

"When are you going to tell me what this crime is I'm supposed to be solving? I've done everything you asked. I lie for you every day. The boys at the Club are my friends."

Alex stood at the window and didn't reply.

"I'm not going to play this game much longer," I said.

I got up to leave, but she grabbed my hand. I could feel her strength. She was so strong I didn't dare move. I knew I would do everything Alex asked of me.

"This isn't a game, Hans. You think the boys at the Club are your friends? Why? Because they fill your glass with champagne and drive you around in their cars? If you go along with it all, then sure, you'll end up with a highly paid job in the City. You'll find a wife through the Club who'll let you do whatever you like with her. You'll think you're entitled to all of it, because you're better than all the rest. But are you, Hans? No, you aren't. Now trust me—or would you rather trust a man like Josh Hartley?"

Josh had three broken ribs; someone had beaten him up on the way home. It wasn't clear whether he would fight in the Varsity match. His ribcage had turned dark blue in places. I wondered how much hatred you had to feel to just go for a person like that.

"I don't want to lie anymore," I said. I wrenched myself free and walked to the door. She didn't make a sound, but when I turned she was standing right there, her face just inches away from mine. Her eyelid was flickering.

"You can't run away," she said.

I fled down the stairs, stumbling and grabbing hold of the banister. The little steps bounced beneath my shoes. I thought of all the young men and women who had run up and down these steps before me. It was a thought that had always given me pleasure. Now it frightened me. Out in the courtyard the rain lashed my face. I was glad Alex couldn't touch me anymore. Sitting in the church tower at boarding school I'd dreamed of adventure, but I was no adventurer.

Before heading out of the gate I turned and peered up through the rain. Alex was standing at her window, watching me.

Peter

Alarm: 7 a.m.

Sport: 50 press-ups, 2 planks 30 seconds each

Masturbation: in the shower

Breakfast: instant noodles with *jiaozi*

Motto of the day: The greatest vulnerability is ignorance.

Aim of the day: Find the Pitt Club bow tie; be the best.

There was a book in the window of Ryder & Amies on King's Parade, under a light blue blazer on a dressmaker's dummy. The book was the size and width of an atlas and thirty centimeters thick. Ryder & Amies was founded in 1864 as a clothing shop and has sold gowns and scarves to university students ever since. The book in the shop window was a compendium of ties. Twelve swatches were glued to each page with the name of the respective club alongside.

I'd been interested in clothes ever since I saw the Sherlock Holmes films. Behind the counter stood a man who I estimated must be at least seventy, but I wasn't very good at guessing white people's ages. The man behind the counter was tall; he had hairs on his nose and a single strand combed over his bald head. His suit was old, and sat well; the elbows had been reinforced with patches.

"Good morning. Could you tell me what that book in the window is?" I asked.

"At last, a sensible question," said the salesman. He reached into the shop window and placed the book on the glass counter.

There were not so many tourists in town at this time of year. The afternoon sun shone through the shop window; the shop itself was almost empty. I saw dust motes spin in the light when the old man opened the book. He leafed through it, stroking the silk. We bent over the pages. He talked about drinking clubs and students who were particularly wild, particularly clever, or particularly good strokes in the rowing eight.

The book had no system. Some of the pages were a mess, loose and yellowed. My heart was pounding; I was waiting for a particular swatch. A few days ago I'd climbed a spruce tree opposite the Pitt Club and had watched to see who went through the door. The members had all been wearing the same dark bow tie, but I hadn't been able to clearly see the pattern. I recognized it here at once, though. Silver, blue and black stripes; beside it was written "P-Club." I stroked my thumb across the silk and looked at the other clubs on the page. In the bottom left-hand corner a strip of silk was missing. Beside it was written "Butterflies."

"Where's the swatch for that one?" I asked.

The old man narrowed his eyes and bent over the page. Without looking up he said that he didn't know, that some clubs were even older than he was.

I had to go to a lecture, on game theory and market models; very important if you want to be an investment banker. I shook the man's hand, inclined my head slightly, thanked him, and left the shop.

Ryder

I work every day of the week, including Sundays, when I do the bookkeeping. In my opinion, a man who isn't working isn't alive. People shouldn't forget what they are. I think the reason England is no longer what it once was is that people have forgotten their place.

I looked through the tie pattern book a while longer. It had to have been about forty years ago, but I remembered it as if it were yesterday: the day a young man with long blond hair had come into the shop and asked to see the book. He'd been friendly and elegant, with very upright bearing. He'd taken the swatch off the page without asking and slipped it into his inside jacket pocket. I remember the yellow butterfly embroidered on the silk, and I remember the man's smile, because he had smiled as he placed an envelope with a large number of twenty-pound notes on the table, saying that the club wanted to avoid publicity in future. I knew then that I was dealing with Old England, and at the same time I knew that I didn't want to know what sort of club this was, or what the swatch was doing in the man's jacket pocket. There were things that were meant for people like me, and this club was not one of them, so my task, the task of a proud English clothier, would be to forget the club and the envelope with the money, and if I didn't succeed in doing that I would remain silent.

Hans

The Viennese tailor came to the Farewell home, to the mansion in Chelsea. He was an Austrian with a blond side-parting and round glasses. Farewell let me make all the decisions, apart from the size of the pockets. A man needed big pockets, he said; you never knew what you might find.

I sat in the library next to Charlotte's room and spent a long time selecting the material. I hadn't known how many different blacks there were. Farewell said that everything was actually gray. There was no such thing as black; it wasn't a real color, it was just an illusion. I decided on a blue-black.

"Like your hair," said Charlotte.

I hadn't noticed that she'd entered the room and sat down on the table behind me. She had a leather suitcase with her.

"We should go down to Somerset," she said. "It's magical at this time of year. You have to see the apple orchards covered in hoarfrost. We could take the Jag and be there in three hours."

Angus Farewell nodded.

"Do you want to?" asked Charlotte.

"Yes," I said.

Charlotte drove slowly and we listened to Belgian chansons. It was an old car, but the stereo was modern. I liked the music. As we came off the motorway and saw the hills of Somerset in the dusk, Charlotte began to sing in a quiet, throaty voice. It was so beautiful I couldn't look at her. Light green fields rolled past the windows and I wished we could drive on forever.

She seemed very familiar with the route. When she turned left down an avenue of bare trees I wondered where we were going. A sign said MANOR HOUSE; it was a phrase I didn't know. The avenue led to a museum in a two-story nineteenth-century mansion with pale yellow walls, two rows of sash windows, and a slate roof. The house had several tall chimneys, and a portico, beside which stood a life-size statue of St Michael with one foot on Satan's head, sword held aloft. I'd never had any interest in museums. I knew Charlotte was studying Art History and I secretly hoped we wouldn't stay long. I wondered what her Swedish boyfriend would think when he found out she was looking at museums in Somerset with me. The thought made me nervous, but ever since we'd got in the car I'd had a buzzing in my chest that I hadn't felt for a very long time.

We walked through the rooms on the ground floor and looked at the paintings on the walls. She stood beside the portrait of a fat, red-haired woman.

"Do you think I look like her?" she asked.

I shook my head. The stairs to the upper floor were out of bounds; a chain with a NO ENTRY sign hung across them. Charlotte climbed over it and ran upstairs. I looked around and couldn't see anyone, so I ran after her, coming to a halt at the top in front of a white-varnished, solid wood door. Charlotte took a key out of her bag.

"What are you doing?" I whispered.

She pushed the door open and took my hand as if it were the most natural thing in the world.

"Didn't Daddy tell you he'd kept the house?"

She curtsied, and started going through the rooms, pulling white sheets off the furniture. The rooms had thirty-foot ceilings; the furniture was of light-colored wood.

"Applewood," Charlotte said.

There were no mattresses on the beds. Every room had a fireplace that looked as if it hadn't seen a fire in a long time. On top of a bureau were photos in silver frames. One showed a married couple with a blonde girl who must have been Charlotte.

* * *

That evening we walked the two miles to the village. In the pub, Charlotte had apple crumble with runny cream and drank cider made of apples grown on the trees behind the manor. I drank black tea and resolved that after this season I would stop boxing. The landlord remembered Charlotte; he talked about how she used to sit on the tractor cab during harvest with her Gameboy in her hand and drink scrumpy straight from the tap. Charlotte gave him an overly large tip.

It was late when we walked back; fog lay over the fields. Charlotte said that if she were alone now she would be scared. She slid an arm around my hips beneath my coat and remarked that I was too thin. Like a greyhound, she said. We walked beside each other, both lost in thought.

"Tell me a story about you, Hans," she said.

I liked it that she called me Hans. Most of the boxers and the men at the Pitt Club just called me Stichler.

The manor house at the end of the road rose up bright against the night sky. I thought about how different Charlotte and I were.

"My parents are dead," I said.

I didn't want to talk about it, and I didn't know why I'd started. My fingers gripped the lining of my coat pockets. I was afraid Charlotte might ask a question I didn't want to answer. But she just walked beside me, saying nothing. I felt her warm arm around my hips and was grateful to have her holding me.

The house was unheated. Charlotte had brought two down-filled sleeping bags in the boot of the Jaguar, which were far too thin. She kissed me on the shoulder, said, "Good night, my little greyhound," and pulled the door closed behind her. The water I washed my face in was so cold my fingertips ached. I laid the sleeping bag on a sofa, then went out onto the balcony. I felt a desire to smoke a cigarette, although I never smoked.

I gazed down for a long time at the apple orchard in the nighttime fog. There were no stars in the sky.

Memories surfaced from that morning, looking at swatches with Angus Farewell. There is such a thing as black, I thought. There is such a thing as the total absence of light.

Late that night, as I lay naked in my sleeping bag, Charlotte came tiptoeing into my room. She wasn't wearing a nightdress.

"It's so cold," she said, and crawled into my sleeping bag. She was soft and warm, and settled down with her back to me. We lay like that for a while.

"Hello, laddie," she said.

"Why do you call me 'laddie'?"

"Because you're a lad compared to me," she said.

I watched my breath stirring the hairs on the back of her neck. We were very close together. I got an erection, and wondered what she was thinking.

"We shouldn't do this," I said.

No idea why I said that.

"I think we should," she said.

She touched me with the back of her head and with her pelvis. I stared at a grandfather clock by the wall that had no hands. Charlotte smelled of cream. Slowly she moved against my skin. My forehead was pressed to the back of her neck; her hair fell in my face. She took my hand and placed it on her hip. I pulled her closer to me.

"Don't be so careful," she said.

She was like a waterfall.

After I came I stayed inside her. I thought about how she moved so confidently in a world that was completely foreign to me: when she'd kissed the antiques dealer on the cheek, when she'd tied my bow tie, when she'd hit me on the back of the head, when she'd come to me tonight on bare feet. But it wasn't this strength that I was attracted to. I could sense her pain. I didn't know where it came from, but it was there, and it attracted me.

I think we found each other in our weakness.

"What are you thinking?" she asked.

"Nothing," I said. I was thinking that her hair curled at the nape of her neck like candyfloss.

"I don't believe you," she said.

"Your hair is like candyfloss." She was sure to laugh at me now.

"That sounds pretty," she said.

From then on I tried to breathe with her, in sync.

Later, her breath coming in little clouds, she told me about her mother. The neurons that controlled her muscles had stopped working when Charlotte was fifteen. Her father had had doctors flown in from Germany and Boston, but the disease was incurable. Charlotte told me how her father had slapped one of the doctors when he'd said there was nothing he could do. Her mother died of heart failure caused by the disease. Her father went back to work the next day.

I held Charlotte, one hand on her belly, and felt her tears falling on my other arm. For a moment I considered telling her about my family, but that night belonged to Charlotte's mother.

"I'm glad you're here," I said.

Charlotte fell asleep on my elbow. After my parents' death I'd thought I could never love again, because the fear of losing someone was too great. I had grown cold inside. Now here was this woman, lying on my arm. I waited for it to get light. When she woke she said she didn't want to go back to Cambridge. I thought about my mission, and the boxing match in four weeks' time, and said nothing.

Charlotte took a shower in the ice-cold water; she left the door open and peered through the glass from time to time to see if I was watching her. She had a small, thin scar on her left breast. I stroked it as she toweled herself dry, and she said that when she was young she'd picked up a rabbit from its cage; the creature had scrabbled with its legs and scratched her. It hadn't been a deep wound, but the scar had remained.

"Do you think I'm fat?" she asked.

"No."

"How old are you?"

"Nineteen."

"You're far too young for me, Greyhound."

"Why?"

She took my head in her hands and kissed me.

"Do you think you could ever find me repulsive?" She looked at me closely. There—in the blink of an eye the darkness had returned.

"No," I said, and kissed her naked belly. "What goes on at the Pitt Club?" I asked.

"Not now," she said, and turned away.

We had breakfast in the village—an omelette, with chives sprinkled on it—then got in the car. Near the sign at the entrance to the village Charlotte stopped by the side of the road, got out and hugged an apple tree. She stood like that for a long time, her cheek against the gray bark.

She's broken, I thought.

Eventually she got back in the car and we drove, too fast, back to London.

Charlotte

My mother wasn't like my father. She believed that unearned wealth could corrupt a child's soul. When I was fourteen she got me a job doing a paper round, although I hadn't asked her to and would far rather have spent all my days riding and eating lemon tarts.

It wasn't actually newspapers I was delivering, but leaflets advertising a Caribbean restaurant that belonged to my nanny's brother, and because hardly anyone living in Chelsea had a taste for black beans I distributed these leaflets once a week in East London, in an area where, back then, there weren't yet any hipsters. I got three pence per leaflet. At first I walked these eastern streets with a pounding heart, but after a few days I lost my inhibitions, and when I finished work I would sit with the big black women in the restaurant kitchen eating all that was put in front of me, listening to reggae and plucking the little feathers from chicken wings, which the women then slid into bubbling fat.

By the time I was sixteen I had plucked countless chickens, slept with the restaurant owner's son, and learned that life had more to offer than lemon tarts. The white façades of Chelsea began to bore me. When I left school I wanted to cut sugarcane on a farm in Jamaica, then study in London and live in the East End, all the things you imagine doing when you're young and think it doesn't matter where you come from.

* * *

Then my mother died. In the last days of her illness she couldn't move her arms or legs any more. A few weeks before the end, when she could still speak, she called me to her bedside one evening and said she was happy with the life she'd led, and could die in peace only if she knew I'd look after my father. He was so alone, she said. I cried for a long time and sat beside her bed all night because I didn't want to let her die. The next day I promised to look after him, and she died less than two months later.

After that my father more or less stopped speaking. The only times he really talked to me were about studying at Cambridge. He told me about the big ball at the end of the academic year and how he would dance at it with me.

I wanted to make him happy again. I applied to Cambridge, and when we heard I'd been accepted I saw him cry for the first time in my life.

I resolved to steer clear of the snobs and lead a normal life. I thought that this was doable.

Hans

Back in Cambridge I spent a few days in the library, but I couldn't concentrate because I kept looking at my mobile, waiting for a message from Charlotte. Then I went to a training camp for the university boxing team. The trainer loaded us all onto a bus and drove us out for the weekend to a barracks half an hour outside town, in the middle of the Fens.

Out of two hundred students who had signed up in October because they wanted to box for the university, seventeen were left.

We jumped rope in an empty hall. A coach in a peaked cap walked up and down between us. We all knew that a year ago he'd still been in jail. From time to time a fast-moving steel rope would clip him and he would ignore it. The students called him Priest. I thought it was a religious reference until someone explained it was the word for the metal club anglers used to hammer fish to death. Priest had spent three years in Whitemoor Prison for robbery; since his release he'd been working for the head boxing coach as an assistant trainer.

The match against Oxford was in three weeks. "Twenty days," bellowed Priest. The ropes hummed. Everyone knew the nine boxers who had made the team would be announced after this weekend. I counted the drops of sweat splashing onto the concrete in front of me. Josh skipped beside me, grimacing. When he saw I was watching him, he winked at me. I thought Josh would probably get to box; even with three broken ribs he was good. There was one boxer, a lightweight, who I was sure would make the team: Michael Foster, a former American paratrooper who seemed to be skipping twice as fast as everyone else. Everyone called him Magic Mike. It was Billy who'd dubbed him that, in reference to a Hollywood film about a male stripper. I was pretty sure Billy had come up with the name because he didn't like Foster. Magic Mike was a devout Baptist who went to church every day, was married, and apparently didn't dance because he believed dancing was an expression of lust and therefore displeasing in the eyes of God.

Billy was skipping heavily. I hoped he'd make it onto the team. The other heavyweight was a Zambian guy; he couldn't box, but he could bench press a hundred and eighty kilos and jump a meter in the air from a standing start.

Beside Priest stood a huge man in uniform. His boot caps shone. I marveled that it was possible for anyone to have such a big head. The man stood with legs akimbo, hands folded behind his back.

"Drop the ropes," he shouted.

His voice was even louder than Priest's. He had a moustache, and his neck was shaved so close he'd scraped off the top layer of skin in places. His uniform was stretched so tightly across his sternum you could see the vest underneath, and his chest was decorated with medals of honor for service in Afghanistan and Iraq. I could see that his hands trembled slightly, though he either kept them in motion or held them behind his back. He took a deep breath.

"Boxers. I am Wing Commander Victor Sprat from the Royal Air Force. That's Wing Commander to you. I'll be leading the training today. We'll be doing the RAF obstacle course. It will be hard. You will feel pain. Ignore it. Pain is not important when you're going into the ring against Oxford in twenty days' time. You'll remember this fight for the rest of your lives. You will want to be able to say on your deathbed: 'I gave that fight everything I had.'

"Come closer, men. You've been waiting for this fight. I've been in more fucking countries than anyone in this room and I'm telling you, not everyone understands English in Afghanistan but they all understand the food chain. The day has come when you've got to decide: are you the predator or the prey? This doesn't mean you go blundering into the ring like it's the Middle Ages. You go in there nice and quiet, then you turn into the ugliest beast there is. Understand?"

"Yes, sir!" yelled Magic Mike.

I stared at the wing commander's neck, where a vein was bulging and throbbing. I hoped that on my deathbed I wouldn't be thinking about a boxing match.

For the next few hours we crawled under barbed wire and shinned up ropes and over walls. The sun shone on the fen outside the barracks; it was a beautiful day. In my mind I was with Charlotte in the old house in Somerset. The wing commander ran up and down beside me, yelling.

I was in the best shape of my life. Only one wall gave me problems because I was too short. Every time, Billy reached down and pulled me up. He didn't look good. He was too heavy for exercises like this; his lungs whistled as he breathed. The Zambian sprang over the wall as if it were a warm-up. The wing commander stood alongside, yelling so loudly in his enthusiasm that strings of saliva flew from his lips. Three hours in, Billy twisted his ankle and was lying there in the mud. The wing commander bent down and screamed in his face, "Come on, Fatso, you don't get this handed to you on a plate like at your poncey uni."

Billy was probably the poorest student I knew. He lived in a tiny room in his college, always wore the same pair of jeans and had a chip butty for dinner almost every evening because it only cost a pound. He once asked me if I could lend him a fiver to pay for the tea we often drank together after training.

The wing commander kicked him in the lateral abdominals with his polished boots and said, "Get up, you spoiled brat. Get up or die."

Billy lay motionless on his back. The wing commander bent down and whispered something in his ear. I thought for a moment he was about to spit on him.

The straight right punch came out of nowhere, catching the wing commander on the chin. He fell forward and hit the ground face first, medals in the mud.

"Boom," said Josh quietly.

Billy left that evening. I walked him to the barracks gate. He was crying.

"Priest wanted me to stay, but the fucking wing commander said if I didn't go he'd have me arrested for hitting an officer. I'm out, Hans. They're not going to let me fight."

I put a hand on his shoulder.

"That was a great punch."

"Do you know what he whispered in my ear?" Billy asked. I shook my head. Billy started to hiccup.

"'Your kind are always the first to die, you rich faggot.'"

I hugged him. Billy held me tight, and I felt his chest heaving with every sob. Out of two hundred students who had signed up in October because they wanted to box for the university, sixteen were left.

Peter

Alarm: 7 a.m.

Sport: 50 press-ups, 2 planks 30 seconds each, 40 squats

Masturbation: once in bed, once in the shower

Breakfast: instant noodles with *jiaozi*

Motto of the day: Opportunities multiply when they are seized.

Aim of the day: Survive the Adonians; make contact with the Pitt
  Club; be the best.

The invitation to the Adonians lay on my desk, handwritten on white card. I had paid another student five hundred pounds to get me on the list. I kept glancing at the invitation as I put on my dinner jacket and fastened the pink bow tie. Pink was appropriate, I thought.

I didn't know what awaited me, only that the Adonians were a club made up of attractive, rich gay men. What I did know was that the president of the Pitt Club was a professor of mathematics who loved colorful dress handkerchiefs and was married to a man. I was certain that I would meet him at the Adonians.

The invitation said the evening would begin with a champagne reception, and dinner would be served at seven-thirty p.m. I entered the Peterhouse Combination Room at 7:28 p.m. in order to appear interesting. Besides, I can't take too much alcohol, and I didn't want to be drunk when the soup was served. The room was illuminated by candles, the tablecloth starched, the air smelling of cedar. I was the only Asian in the room, and the only man in a pink bow tie.

The man beside me was wearing glittering cufflinks. They were hideous.

"Nice cufflinks," I said.

He introduced himself as Gilly. The cufflinks had originally been women's diamond earrings that he'd had refashioned by an Indian jeweler in London. We talked a little about our bespoke tailors. When Gilly put his hand on my knee I wondered whether I should smash in his front teeth with my bread plate. For the time being I decided against.

We ate a lukewarm spinach soup, cured pigeon, lamb with green beans, and Eton Mess, a mixture of strawberries, meringue, and cream; however, I was already so drunk by then that I barely registered dessert. I had spotted the math professor at the other end of the room.

When the catering staff brought in the port, a gray-haired man stood up and gave a speech full of metaphors that probably only British people understand. I endeavoured to laugh at the right moments. At the end of the speech the gray-haired man said we could now either go upstairs and drink more Bardolino or go out into the college garden and enjoy the pleasures of Uranus. Everybody laughed; I slapped my knees, wondering whether other people did that as well or whether it was just a manner of speaking when they said a person laughed so hard he slapped his thighs.

A little later I saw the professor of mathematics going out through a door that led to the garden.

I thought of a quotation from Clausewitz I'd once learned by heart for my exams back home in Beijing: "The end for which a soldier is recruited, clothed, armed, and trained, the whole object of his sleeping, eating, drinking, and marching, is simply that he should fight at the right place and the right time." This sentence had so captured me that I had downloaded the complete works of Clausewitz from the internet and learned individual passages by heart. The only thing that bothered me was his death. A pitiful demise, getting cholera from a spoiled piece of Prague ham and falling off a latrine in Breslau a week later, completely dehydrated. Apart from that, I had the feeling that I, Peter Wong, and Carl von Clausewitz had a great deal in common.

I went out into the garden. The professor was leaning back against the trunk of an oak. A young man was busy sucking his member.

"Professor, I would like to put myself forward for membership of the Pitt Club," I said.

The professor studied me from head to toe and smiled. The student gave me a little yellow flask.

"Inhale deeply," said the professor.

I inhaled and knew that it was all OK; I repeated the same sentence in my head over and over again on an endless loop and felt extremely clever. I had not been gay until that night, and I will kill anyone who claims I am in future. I didn't enjoy it, but I knew I was doing the right thing. "War is never an isolated act."

Charlotte

I put on a pair of ballet tights. It was several years since I'd danced, but I had vivid memories of the Spanish dance teacher my father used to invite to come to the house once a week to teach me and three of my friends. Back then I wanted to go to a normal dance school and dance with boys, like all the other girls, but Father said, "You're not like all the other girls." The advantage of having lessons with my girlfriends was that I learned to dance the men's steps and to lead.

I sat on the top step outside Hans's room; I'd spread my coat over my legs to keep warm. As I waited I thought about our trip to Somerset. He wasn't like anyone else. Perhaps that was why I liked him. He was only nineteen, quiet, never funny, too short, shy; yet he made me feel a way I'd almost forgotten. There were moments when he was miles away, even though he was sitting right next to me; most of the time he seemed to be only half there. I'd gone to his bed because I felt like it; I didn't think emotions were involved. He'd held me, and for the first time in ages I'd felt safe, but at the same time I knew he and I could never be happy together.

The following day I'd called Magnus, met him in Starbucks at King's Cross and told him I didn't love him. He didn't cry. His blond hair sat perfectly. He drank a Frappuccino and said that that was regrettable.

Hans came up the stairs, drenched in sweat to the tips of his hair. He wasn't bleeding this time. I heard myself sigh.

Every time he came back from boxing training I was afraid his nose would be broken. If he'd been hit hard he would put an ice pack on his face and smile. It was a part of him I would never understand.

When I saw him I felt a tingling in my lungs as if I had breathed in smoke. I kissed him on the lips. He tasted of salt. I felt the heat of his skin.

"Hello, Hans. Do you want to learn to dance?"

"Hello, Charlotte Farewell," he said. I liked his accent.

He showered and put on a tracksuit. It had CAMBRIDGE UNIVERSITY AMATEUR BOXING CLUB written on the back in turquoise letters. I could see how proud he was. He'd made it onto the team. Father still wore his old, faded team tracksuit; he'd had the cuffs replaced twice.

I took Hans by the hand. His palms grew moist; in any other man that would have made me cringe. We went to my flat. I pushed the table and a couple of armchairs aside and stood in front of him in the middle of the room. I took his right hand and placed it on my shoulder blade. Beneath the polyester of his tracksuit top I could feel his shoulder, hard as wood.

"Can you hear the rhythm?" I asked.

He nodded. I didn't explain much, I just danced. Light-footed, a simple, slow tango. Hans took small steps; he was better than I'd expected. He danced in white socks; he didn't notice that he was following and I was leading. I felt his palms grow damp again and looked him in the eye. After a few minutes he stopped, still looking at me.

"What did they do to you?" he asked.

I dropped his hand and sat down at the table. He sat beside me and looked at the tabletop. He would never look at me the same way again after this.

I told him everything.

The envelope with the butterfly seal was in my desk in another room, along with the doctor's report. I fetched them both.

I told the story as if it were a stranger's; that made it easier. Hans kept nodding as he read the doctor's report.

"I'm not a victim," I said.

He went on nodding, as if my words hadn't reached him. He took the card out of the envelope and looked at it for a long time.

"It's nice handwriting," he said.

"Do you find me repulsive now?"

He kissed my fingertips and shook his head. "You're the best thing about this place."

I knew he was saying it to make me feel better.

"I've read that most women feel guilty somehow, after something like this," he said.

"Why should I feel guilty?"

"I didn't mean it like that. Sorry."

Tears rolled down my cheeks.

"What does this change?" I asked.

"Nothing."

"Don't be stupid. It changes everything."

He looked as if he were searching for words and failing to find them. How much harder must it be to have this conversation in a foreign language? I put my hand on his cheek.

"I showed you the woman's steps."

"I know," he said.

"You don't understand, Hans. I was the one leading. You were dancing the tango the wrong way round."

He'd known all along. I could see it in his eyes.

Charlotte

The morning before the night that changed everything, I was nineteen years old and at the end of my first year. I'd got up early that day because I wanted to go riding. In my pigeonhole in the porters' lodge there was a thick envelope with no name on it. I turned the envelope over and saw on the back a yellow wax seal stamped with the shape of a butterfly.

I pushed my little finger under the flap and opened the letter without breaking the seal. Inside was a card on which was written, in blue ink and rounded letters, "Charlotte Farewell, we are expecting you. Tonight is your night."

When I read those lines, I laughed. I wanted a boyfriend, and the note sounded as if it had been written by a man; the writing looked like a man's, anyway, though I might have been wrong. I'd been invited to a party at the Pitt Club that evening; a girlfriend had begged me to take her, and it was the last big party before the summer holidays, so I'd accepted. The letter probably had something to do with the party, I thought.

That evening I put on one of my black dresses and a pair of ballet tights, because they were tougher than ordinary ones and made your legs look good. I didn't want them to ladder tonight. My friend came round; we drank vodka with cranberry juice and ice and talked about who might be behind the butterfly seal, and how my friend was going on holiday to the

Maldives in the summer and was going to do an internship at *Vogue* afterwards; her father knew the editor-in-chief. We drank half the bottle and listened to the ice cubes clinking in our glasses.

Outside my window Chapel Court lay bathed in moonlight, paved with little stones. I hadn't anticipated it, but I was now so happy to have the chance to study here that I sometimes felt I wanted to hug a tourist. It was a warm evening and the air was soft, the way it usually only is in August.

"I'm so grateful to the universe for everything," I said.

"Let's party," said my friend.

The next morning I woke up in a field behind my college. I lay there like a piece of driftwood, unable to remember a thing. When I sat up I saw the blood that had soaked the ballet tights all the way down to the knees.

The morning after that night four years ago, I dug my fingers into the grass and closed my eyes. I hoped that the grass would stop spinning. After a few minutes I got to my feet, walked back to my college on trembling legs and asked the porter for a spare key to my room. He glanced at my torn dress and looked at me as if I were a prostitute.

When I got there I went to the bathroom and threw up in the loo. I washed my mouth out and propped myself up on the basin. I lay down on the floor and tried to remember the previous night. I could see into my room through the open door; the two wine glasses from which we'd drunk the vodka were on the windowsill, but the alcohol couldn't have knocked me out like that. My memory took me as far as the Club, then it broke off. I felt as if I'd been cauterized inside.

I crawled back into my room, found my phone, and Googled "Cambridge rape." The third hit took me to the site www.cambridgecrisis.org.uk. It said: *Wrap up in something warm and have a hot drink, which will help if you are in shock.* I picked up a sweater, pressed my face into it, and hoped the porter wouldn't hear the screams.

Victims of rape were advised to report immediately to the police. *Try not to eat, smoke, wash yourself, change your clothes, go to the toilet, or clean up the scene of the crime. Don't go to hospital first; go straight to the police.* The police would contact the forensics department at Peterborough City Hospital and arrange an examination that would document all traces of rape. The victim would have to file a report.

The victim. That was me.

I curled up on the floor. I remembered watching a documentary about women in Rwanda who'd become pregnant as a result of rape. The program was called something like *The Enemy in the Child.* The women were ashamed because they hadn't fought back, and because they thought they had somehow provoked the perpetrators to do what they had done.

There must still be flakes of his skin under my fingernails, I thought. I clung to a single thought: I would not be a victim.

I knew the number of the taxi firm by heart. I wanted to go to hospital and get medicine to prevent possible HIV infection. And I needed the morning-after pill as well. I would get through this on my own. I didn't need the police, I needed a doctor. Something was wrong. The bleeding wouldn't stop.

Billy

There was an unfamiliar but blissful smell that evening: soy sauce, fat cooling in the deep-fat fryer, sweat, beer, smoke, and blood.

I was sitting in the kitchen of a Chinese restaurant called Sing Sing in Hackney, East London, bleeding from the mouth. No idea where exactly the blood was coming from. I'd just had my first fight in the dining room. The tables had been pushed aside and a ring set up in the middle. The kitchen had been converted into a changing room.

A friend had told me about these fights. They took place at night; there was no doctor and no official weigh-in, because the fights were illegal. You wrote a few e-mails to an address your friend had given you, and you met a man who wore a trenchcoat and smelled of peanut butter. The meeting took place in a café in London, and the man looked like an insurance salesman but didn't talk like one. He said he would find an opponent. He explained that fights took place in warehouses, in restaurants, in backyards in summer, sometimes in private flats. The spectators and the fighters received a text shortly beforehand giving them the place and time. It all sounded very dubious and I knew it wasn't a sensible thing to do. But if a boxer didn't box, what was he? Something like alcohol-free beer or decaffeinated coffee. I didn't want to be like that. For a long time all I knew was what I didn't want to be. That evening I knew what I did want to be.

My opponent was experienced; he must have weighed at least a hundred and twenty kilos and he called himself "The Baker." It sounded daft, but you just had to look at the man to see that he was far from amusing.

The fight lasted more than six rounds. I knew I would lose, but I'd been training all year and I wanted a fight. You go into the ring and all you can make out are silhouettes, no faces. The main thing is just to get through it; that's the only thought in your head. In the front row was a woman in a bikini who was staring at me and stroking a pug on her lap. Why was she wearing a bikini? The brass bell was dull; I liked the sound. I took a lot of punishment; the referee should have stopped the fight. In the breaks between each round I stared at the pug.

After the fight, a few more boxers were warming up in the kitchen; everyone was preoccupied with himself.

I'd wanted to take Hans with me, but I hadn't dared because I didn't want to lose in front of him. He was so good.

Recently I'd often wondered whether Hans had turned into someone else. He went to the Pitt Club a lot, cooked meals with Josh, and had started wearing fancy shirts and leather shoes every day. He looked like a twat now. I somehow got the feeling he was embarrassed when we met. Perhaps I'd been wrong about him.

I showered in a side room off the kitchen. A man had given me a hundred pounds cash for the fight; I was planning to spend the rest of the evening in the company of various alcoholic drinks. As the water started falling onto my head, rinsing the Vaseline off my eyebrows, I realized how good I felt.

My head was ringing a bit, but I'd held my ground. I'd landed a few punches against The Baker. My senses had been heightened in the ring: I'd been able to smell the pug, the cigarette smoke, the alcohol fumes; it was insane. I knew that none of the spectators were thinking about whether any of us were gay. Poor, rich—didn't matter. Tonight I was a boxer. While we were still in the ring The Baker had said I was a bloody hard little fucker. No idea what he meant by that, but it sounded like a compliment.

I went back into the restaurant in jeans and a flannel shirt. I didn't want to watch the other fights because I was too tired and the people in this place made me nervous. They were smoking and yelling at the boxers.

"Hey, Billy. Bloody good fight, my son."

It was Priest, my coach. He was leaning against the wall by the entrance, smelling of beer and fish and chips.

"What are you doing here?"

"I'm a boxing coach. Boxing coaches watch boxing matches. Fancy a beer?"

He patted my face, quite hard, and we left the restaurant. The lights were off, the curtains drawn; from the outside the restaurant looked as if it were closed.

"The other guy must have had at least ten fights already," said Priest.

I looked at him: leather jacket, slightly drunk, shoulders hunched, chin always lowered. I'd heard from one of the former boxers that Priest had once been England's great light-heavyweight hope, but when he was twenty-five he had an accident. He'd wanted to go to a disco but the bouncers wouldn't let him in because he was wearing cream-colored shoes. He decided to climb in over the roof. He was working as a roofer at the time; heights didn't bother him. He climbed up a fire escape, removed a couple of pantiles, and got into the building from above. Then he slipped, fell three meters, landed on his back, shattered a vertebra in his neck and broke his hip. That was the story, anyway. His friends thought he'd gone home. No one heard him shouting. Two days later a cleaning lady found him when she went up to the attic to get some bleach. Priest had ripped the thermal insulation out of the wall and wrapped himself in it so he didn't freeze to death. It was January. When he arrived in intensive care he was incoherent and his body temperature was 31 degrees Celsius; they said he'd stopped shivering hours earlier. His doctor said he shouldn't box anymore because he ran the risk of injuring the cervical vertebra again and ending up in a wheelchair. The following year Priest raided his first kiosk. His weapon of choice was a vacuum cleaner tube.

How I would have loved to walk into the ring against Oxford with this man at my side.

We went to a pub beside the railway. Priest said he knew the area pretty well; he used to do business here. He gave the woman behind the bar a kiss on the cheek and called her Mimi; she was old, peroxide blonde, and looked like a prostitute. He ordered three beers and three gins and told Mimi I'd just had my first fight.

"D'you win?" she asked.

I think it was Nietzsche who once said the best thing about a great victory is that it rids the victor of the fear of defeat. Somehow that's true of the loser as well.

I stared into my beer.

"Yes," said Priest, "but not on points."

We sat there in front of our glasses. I thought about the fight and tried to put the individual rounds in order. In my memory it was all a mixture of sweat, anger, and fear. I drank and looked through the glass. Priest appeared to be thinking of nothing at all, which I thought must be an enviable state.

"D'you know why it's so hard to make boxers out of you lot?" he asked, as the night wore on. I'd never considered it. Priest took a large swig of his beer.

"You got it all. You got money, houses, gorgeous girl-friends, healthy bodies, you're all at that fucking uni, in a couple of years you'll all be driving Bentleys." I wanted to say something, but Priest went on talking.

"But you ain't got no anger. You can't teach people that. I had anger, still got it. The German's got anger, but he's not right in the head. You got anger too, son; you're not like those spoiled softies, I saw that tonight. Win, lose—fuck it. You got fire in your belly. I wanted you to be on the team, almost came to blows with the boss about it. Sorry, mate."

I leaned back, tipping my bar stool. Priest went on staring straight ahead.

"I don't give a fuck that you like men, Billy."

I breathed in through my nose and out through my mouth, trying not to cry, but my eyes were glistening.

"Is that the reason?"

Priest slammed his glass down on the table.

"Fuck, yeah, that's the reason. The boss never liked you; now you've given him a reason. You would have destroyed that Oxford bastard. The boss is an arsehole. Total pigot."

"Bigot," I said, and was immediately ashamed of myself.

"Yeah, fuck you—bigot, then, who gives a shit. Don't put on your fancy student airs round here."

I slapped his cloth cap. "Thanks, Priest."

I didn't need the team to be happy; The Baker had shown me that. I would watch the match against Oxford; I wanted to be there when Hans won, and I wanted to see the rest of the team lose.

Priest paid for the drinks. "I'll get it," I said, but he just smiled and put a couple of notes on the bar.

I gave Mimi a kiss on the cheek. "I'm off soon," she said in my ear. I winked at her and left.

We staggered down the road for a bit, arm in arm. Priest was singing a song in a broad Cockney accent; I didn't understand all of it.

"I'm gonna kip round the corner. Still got a few little pigeons in the loft here," he said.

"Pigeons?"

"Los Taubos," said Priest.

I walked alone through the streets of London, spat a little blood out onto the pavement and felt good. I was a boxer, a man. A slight drizzle set in, the best weather in the world. I was carrying my sports bag with my damp gloves inside.

Magic Mike

Seven o'clock, the morning of the match. I liked to go to King's College Chapel before the tourists arrived. I'd been waiting for this day for weeks. I was looking forward to the fight, but right now, more than anything, I was looking forward to eating. I'd lost seven kilos in the past four months. I was sixty kilos at a height of six foot one. The last few weeks all I'd had to eat was boiled chicken breast and eggs. I started salivating at the thought of a slice of toast. The last few days I'd passed out a couple of times; once I woke up on the living room floor. I'd dropped the last two kilos through dehydration. In the past twenty hours I'd had just two sips of water and had spent a lot of time in the sauna. My head was throbbing, but I weighed 59.8 kilos. Amen.

That morning I'd looked in the mirror and all I'd seen was a skeleton. Now I was wearing a black suit and the boxing club tie.

I knelt on the flagstones in front of a painting. The cold floor hurt my knees a bit; that was good. The painting showed the newborn Jesus on his mother's lap. Jesus looked all plump and cute. I didn't like that. I didn't like all the modern church stuff that made Jesus come across like a communist and God like the Coca-Cola Santa Claus, but it was quiet here in the morning and a bad church was better than no church at all.

I believe in an avenging God. Back home in Florida I went to a church housed in what used to be the go-cart track, opposite a bookie for greyhound races. When the preacher found out the walls were fireproof he started burning man-sized wooden crosses during services. I thought it was awesome. He preached clutching a wooden hammer he'd bought in a hardware store, shouting through the smoke that God would cast all people who disobeyed His word into the eternal

flames. The preacher slammed the hammer down on the altar;
I felt the heat and knew there was a God.

God was with me when I stormed Fallujah. Once, two
men in front of me stepped on mines and lost their legs. They
smelled like grilled meat but a bit sweeter. Since then I've lost
my appetite for steak. I fought in Iraq for a whole year and
the only injuries I sustained were a couple of scratches from
kicking in wooden doors. Afterwards I knew that I would
dedicate my life to God in gratitude. I was writing the last
chapter of my dissertation about the Vatican's influence on
Ferdinand Maximilian Joseph Maria of Austria, the man who
was emperor of Mexico for a couple of years, cool guy. After
university I was going to go back to the States and go into
politics.

I didn't like the boxing team. Priest was a criminal, Josh
a psycho, Billy a fag and Stichler a Kraut. They were a bunch
of weirdos.

And why did they call me Magic Mike? I watched the
film and all I saw was a musclebound homo dancing around
waving a welding torch. At moments like these I wanted to
give up boxing, but then I realized God had given me this
team as a test.

In Iraq I'd learned parts of the Bible by heart, from an old
translation Reverend Whitler had given me. It was a leather-
bound edition. I was holding it in my hand that morning.

My father had told me that Reverend Whitler had recently
burned a Koran during a service and had had to leave town

as a result, but I don't know whether that's true. All I know is what it says in Hebrews 12: *Let us lay aside every weight, and the sin which doth so easily beset us, and let us run with patience the race that is set before us, looking unto Jesus the author and finisher of our faith.*

I would run the race that was set before me. I would fight the good fight. I stood up; a sprinkling of dust clung to my knees. Outside the chapel I turned my on cell phone and found a message from Priest: *Ready, Magic?*

I was ready. I'd always won all my fights. In the army in Iraq, and in the boxing ring: seven victories, no defeats. The weigh-in was at midday. I would walk into the ring tonight and win. Beforehand I would eat five cheese sandwiches and a big bowl of Cocoa Krispies. Right now I wanted to go home and sleep with my wife, maybe father my first son, God willing.

Billy

The morning smelled of the dry wood of the wall paneling, of the unwashed clothes on my floor, of being at home.

I was still half-asleep when I heard the phone. I reached down beside the bed and pulled it out of my jeans. I felt a bit dizzy.

Priest's voice on the line was soft, which made me uneasy. I'd never heard him like this. It was the day of the Varsity match; my ticket was pinned to the board above my bed. He was talking too fast; he said a friend who worked with the English boxing association had told him there would be unannounced doping tests at the weigh-in today. The Zambian guy was pumped up to the eyeballs with clenbuterol and there was no other heavyweight, only me. Priest asked if I was at fighting weight.

"Wait, wait, wait. What?"

I dropped my arm in astonishment. The phone lay on my blanket. I looked at the clock on the display. Three and a half hours till weigh-in. I was too light; I knew it. Since the fight in London I'd eaten almost nothing but beer and bananas because I hadn't had the appetite for anything else. I didn't have a clue what I weighed.

I hung up without saying goodbye, and immediately regretted it. I pulled my laptop out from under the bed, Googled "clenbuterol" and read that it makes the body burn a lot of fat very fast, and that it was actually a medicine used to treat people with asthma. And as a labor suppressant in cows.

The phone rang. Priest just went on talking. I interrupted him.

"Does the head coach know?"

"He begged me to call you. Billy, this is your chance. You hear me, son? We're gonna box tonight. Fucking hell, we're gonna box."

A ray of light poked through the curtains. I looked at my tiny room and the sloping wall, on which I'd hung a rainbow flag, the ends tacked to the wood with drawing pins. Daft, I know.

Why would anyone need more than a few square meters to live in?

I'd been dreaming for years of bringing home the boxers' light-blue blazer. The red lion on the breast pocket. My father would be proud. I thought about my ringwalk music.

Three and a half hours later I was standing on the scales at the venue. The Oxford boxers were waiting in a corner of the room. None of them glanced over. I'd weighed eighty-eight kilos that morning—not nearly enough. Priest said I should drink two liters of water so I wouldn't be too light, or it would give my opponent an advantage. Heavyweight means the boxers have to weigh less than ninety-one kilos. Most weigh exactly that. Priest said energy was mass times speed and talked about psychological warfare. I drank until nothing more would go in, after which I weighed 90.5 kilos.

After the weigh-in I went to the toilet in a side room off the hall. When I opened the door again a young man in a dark blue Oxford tracksuit was standing in front of me looking the opposite of relaxed. He was almost as tall as me and much broader. He looked like a weightlifter. His biceps made me think of honeydew melons. He planted himself in front of me, shoulders rising and falling with each breath.

"Are you the heavyweight?" he asked.

"Yes." It was a quiet yes. I felt my knees turn to jelly. The man was breathing right in my face.

"I'm gonna smash your skull tonight," he said. His accent sounded Australian.

"Let me through," I said.

The heavyweight didn't move. His breath smelled as if a couple of papayas were rotting in his stomach. I knew that boxing matches were won in the mind, at least that was what people said, and if it were true, then right now my opponent was winning.

I'd never picked a fight in a pub and I was ashamed of having hit the wing commander. I'd written to him to apologize; I didn't like uncontrolled violence. I'd always seen boxing as a sport—violent, but controlled, disciplined. Now, though, I would have to go against my principles.

I grabbed the Oxford boxer by the neck and flung my whole weight against him, shoulder to chest, shoving him all the way across the room to the washbasin where I pushed his neck down and bent over right in his face. His eyes were wide; he hadn't reckoned with this.

"See you tonight," I said. I let go and walked out of the door.

Outside I shoved my trembling hands in my pockets and left the building as if nothing had happened. Gray clouds were gathering in the sky. I felt like having a beer. Or three.

Hans

Charlotte was waiting for me on the college roof overlooking Chapel Court. You weren't allowed on the roof; perhaps that was why she'd wanted to go up there. She was sitting on a blanket, her skin covered in little raindrops; she looked as if she'd already been there for a while. That morning she'd told me to meet her on the roof, and asked if she could accompany me to the boxing hall afterwards. It felt a bit melodramatic to me—it was only a boxing match—but I'd said yes. I couldn't stop thinking about how wounded she had seemed when she told me about being raped. I wondered what it meant for us. I opened a plastic umbrella over her head and sat down beside her.

I'd thought a lot about the Pitt Club in the last few days. I was disgusted that its members had hugged me, that I'd drunk with them from the same glass.

When she'd finished telling me her story she had put her hand over her mouth, the way people do when they're scared. I couldn't stop thinking about that gesture.

Alex had told me right at the beginning that my mission had something to do with the boxers at the Club. If I wanted them to respect me, I had to win the match against Oxford. This was about more than just a blue blazer.

After the weigh-in that morning Priest had told me my opponent had once been the junior champion of Scotland, but that it shouldn't make me nervous. I wondered what it would be like to lose.

My mother's necklace was in my tracksuit pocket. I'd taken it off after my first visit to the Pitt Club because I felt uncomfortable wearing it while pretending to be someone I wasn't. Today I'd taken it out of the shoebox where I kept my passport and a few photos of my parents.

Charlotte's cool, damp hair stuck to my shaven neck. The rules of the Amateur Boxing Association of England required fighters to be clean-shaven. I stroked her arm; when I touched a spot below her elbow, she flinched. I pushed up her sleeve. She struggled to pull away, but I held on tightly to her wrist. There was a deep cut on her forearm; it was freshly healed and looked as if it had been made with a razor. At boarding school I'd known a boy who used to cut his arms; I knew what the wounds looked like. The boy was called Ferdinand; when he was twenty-two he drove his father's Porsche into Lake Starnberg and drowned. The obituary said it was an accident.

Tears were pouring down Charlotte's face. "I can't do this any more," she said.

I wrapped my coat around her shoulders and took her in my arms. I could be strong for both of us until I found out who had hurt her. I couldn't conceive of what would happen after that. We sat there for a long time. Her breathing slowly grew calmer. The rain got heavier, drumming on the umbrella. I hoped there would be lightning.

I took the necklace out of my tracksuit pocket and put it in Charlotte's hand.

"Please wear it this evening. It belonged to my mother."

Charlotte shook her head and moved her lips as if she were trying to say something. Her fingers closed silently on the necklace.

"I want to get away from here," she said.

I looked up into the clouds and thought of her pressing her face to the bark of the apple tree. Perhaps I should have told her how, when I was a child, I liked nothing better than to run off and climb the poplar, or how I used to run up the steps of the church tower at boarding school and sit up there all on my own. All my life I had run away, done what other people had told me. I wasn't going to run tonight.

"I'll find them," I said.

The clock on St. John's College Chapel had no hands, like the grandfather clock in the house in Somerset. I wondered whether this was significant.

Charlotte carried my sports bag as we walked to the venue. We went through the porters' lodge; the porters gave me the thumbs-up, but judging by their expressions they weren't too bothered. That morning I'd found a card in my pigeonhole: *Knock him dead. Wishing you the best of luck, Alex.*

The first spectators were waiting outside the hall. The fights would start in two hours. When the people saw my team tracksuit they stood aside and made a corridor for us. Someone shouted something; someone else slapped me on the shoulder.

Charlotte and I looked at each other and nodded before I walked on alone through the door of the hall. Charlotte was different this evening, perhaps because of the fight. I could smell the carpet in the entrance; it had been sprayed with something lemon scented. The fights were taking place in the old Corn Exchange. A sign above the door read SHOWTIME. I didn't know where the dressing room was, so I went into the auditorium and contemplated the empty plastic chairs. A little light fell through the narrow windows near the ceiling; the rest of the room was in semi-darkness. In the middle stood a boxing ring.

I sat on the edge of the ring and lay down with my back on the mat. I thought of the cut in Charlotte's arm, closed my eyes, and for some inexplicable reason fell asleep, waking only when the spotlights were switched on. I've noticed since that in certain situations I tend to become calm while other people are practically crawling up the walls. I stared into the light, trying to count the lamps, but they were so bright I got confused each time I reached the middle of the lighting bar. I wasn't sure, but I thought one of the lights wasn't working.

Hans

The dressing room was on the first floor. The boxers were sitting on chairs lined up against the wall. Josh was watching a film on his iPad, Magic Mike was eating Cocoa Krispies from a plastic bowl. The coaches were pacing up and down, saying things nobody heard: "Always use your full reach" and "This is what you've been waiting for, lads."

After I'd changed I went downstairs, positioned myself behind a curtain and peered out at the crowd gathering in the hall. The curtain was red velvet; it was soft against my cheek. The venue was full: 1,300 spectators, sold out. It was warm and smelled of popcorn and beer. In the third row was Angus Farewell, wearing his light-blue blazer; Charlotte sat beside him in a long-sleeved black dress that was too thin for a cold March evening. The material concealed the cut on her arm. She was wearing my mother's necklace around her neck.

The first match went to Cambridge. Theo, a black guy who was our featherweight, moved as if he'd been boxing his entire life. I saw the lust for blood and pain in the spectators' faces. I would never understand why people watched boxing matches.

1:0.

The second boxer was Magic Mike. He walked in to a Wagner aria. A few spectators laughed. As he walked through the crowd to the ring, I saw how thin he was. He'd made his body his enemy.

I don't know whether there's such a thing as a soul, but if there is, I believe that boxing can change it.

"It's Magic Mike," some of the lads shouted from the stands. He knelt down in a corner of the ring and crossed himself three times. His expression was serious. The bell rang; his opponent floored him with his first left hook and broke his jaw. It happened so fast that I stepped forward through the curtain, but no one was looking in my direction. They were all looking at Magic Mike, who was kneeling on all fours with no expression at all any more. Saliva poured down his chin. The referee counted him out.

1:1.

Magic Mike walked straight up to me as he came out of the ring. He stopped and stared at me as if seeing me for the very first time. His jaw hung slack.

Priest put his hand on my shoulder.

"Quick, son, warm up," he said.

I punched the mitts a few times. I was in a cold sweat. I didn't like the spectators because they were so loud. I jumped rope for a few minutes, staring at the fire extinguisher on the wall. A sign beside it said IN EMERGENCY, SMASH GLASS.

Steve, our light welterweight, lost on points.

1:2.

I'd spent a long time thinking about what music would feel right. I'd even asked Charlotte, but regretted it when she suggested a chanson. I didn't listen to music; I jogged without music, boxed without music. There'd been music at my parents' funeral. I asked Priest if I could walk in in silence, and he just shrugged.

I walked into the ring without any music. I didn't cheer, didn't raise my arm, just walked into the ring. Hardly anyone clapped; it was as if they didn't see me. That was good. I slipped between the ropes, bowed to the referee, and looked my opponent in the eye.

He looks like an old man. Priest saw in his fight record that the Scot's nineteen years old, but he's already balding on top. The bell rings. *Ding ding.* My opponent throws a combination. He's better, he's simply better, I sense it right away. One of the first punches breaks my nose. Blood runs down my throat; it tastes of copper. How do I know what copper tastes like? Work at range now. The shortest distance between two points is a straight line. Left, left, right. The Scot is too fast.

End of round one. Priest puts an ice pack on my head and gives me a pep talk. He smears half a pot of Vaseline on my face and plugs up my nostrils, which stops the bleeding for a few seconds.

I'm back in the wine cellar at boarding school. Father Gerald is smiling. *Do the opposite of what your opponent expects.*

He used to say that all the time. He had such a lovely laugh. Why did I never write to him?

I can see the night sky through the windows in the roof of the hall. Lightning at last.

In the next round I take up a position in a corner of the ring. The dead zone, my first coach used to call it.

"Get out of the corner!"

No idea who's shouting that; doesn't matter.

The Scot throws a couple of straight punches to my face. He's good; I want to tire him out. I leap forward, grab him and fling him onto the ropes. Now he's the one in the corner. This is my chance. He dodges; I punch and punch. I feel his cheekbone through my gloves. I lean over him in the corner. Hang on to my neck, you're not getting out of here. I can smell the shampoo he used to wash his tonsure. Apple scented. I hit him in the stomach and the ribs. I feel the heat. I hit. I hit. I hit.

In the second break the head coach is jumping up and down, waving a towel. I peer through the ropes. Angus is standing right beside the ring; he gives me a nod.

I've never been so tired. I could fall to the floor and it would all be over. The Scot's first left hits me smack in the face; he's still fighting. I hear my nasal bone dislocate. The sound seems to come from right inside my skull. Halfway through the round the Scot's on the ropes again. I throw hooks and upper cuts and breathe through my open mouth. With every punch I yell out my anger. When the bell rings I know that I've won. The referee yanks my arm in the air. It's over. No one can take this away from me. Victory. I should be happy.

2:2.

I step out of the ring. My nose feels fat. On the way back to the dressing room Angus is standing there; he puts both hands on my shoulders.

Hans

When I came out of the shower I was still sweating. I'd stuck rolled-up toilet paper up my nostrils. Someone told me Josh had won. Knockout in the first round. When I left the dressing room it was 4:4.

Now Billy had to win. His music was booming from the speakers so loudly that many in the hall were flinching: the sound of a trumpet. One thousand three hundred spectators were staring at the red velvet curtain, waiting for the Cambridge University heavyweight. The room was hot; nobody was sitting in their chair any more. They were all clapping hard and shouting Billy's name.

Billy

"You hear those people out there, my son? They're calling for you. I want you to think of all the people in your life who've done you wrong. You're gonna hit every one of 'em tonight in this ring. Hear me, Billy? Now get out there. You show 'em, Billy, come on, lad, you show 'em!"

Hans

Billy strode forward through the curtain. He was holding a flag with both hands, stretched out above his head. It was the rainbow flag from the wall of his room. He gazed up into the light. All the other boxers had walked through the curtain and headed straight for the ring. The coaches had told us the referees didn't like it when we put on a show. Billy stood in front of the curtain, drinking it all in, holding the flag up high. Priest stood beside him and raised his left fist towards the ceiling, his right hand on Billy's shoulder. The spectators started clapping in a hard, slow, deliberate rhythm. The noise in the hall was deafening.

Billy's opponent was already in the ring, running from corner to corner. Someone had told me he was from Samoa and was actually a rugby player. Billy walked up to him, stepping lightly. I realized how much I'd missed Billy. In the past few weeks I'd spent more time with Josh than with him; I'd felt bad about it, but I knew it was important, because Josh knew everyone in the Pitt Club. When the fight began, Priest wrapped the rainbow flag around his shoulders. The head coach yelled at him. Priest's right arm shot down; the movement was fast and precise, nimble as a boxer who had once been good and knew how to use his hands. He grabbed the head coach by the jaw and hissed something in his face.

Billy's hands were flashing in the spotlights. The Samoan leapt forward and swung at him; Billy dodged the blows as if he could see them all coming. In the first break Priest stood in front of him in the corner. Billy didn't sit on the stool. The two of them stood facing each other in silence, breathing calmly. I moved closer. I remembered how Billy had been beaten up in the Pitt Club at the start of the year, and wondered when he'd learned to box like that. At the end of the break Priest said just one sentence: "I'm so proud of you, my son."

The sweat glistened on Billy's skin. At the start of the second round he floored his opponent with a straight right. All I could see were the whites of the Samoan's eyes. The ringside doctor leapt into the ring and pulled his tongue out of his throat—he'd swallowed it.

5:4.

Victory. Billy had done it. I felt so light at that moment. I climbed into the ring and hugged him. We probably said something to each other, but I don't remember what, only the spotlights, all of which were shining.

Someone passed up a bottle of champagne through the ropes; Josh poured it over Billy's head. I saw Priest down below, outside the ring; he took the bucket of water, the towels and Billy's colorful flag and walked out of the hall.

Alex

The ring stood in the middle of the hall, like an altar. A person is sacrificed; the crowd cheers. And they say I'm the crazy one.

I was sitting in the back row in the second block on the left.

The spectators left their seats. I stayed sitting. He was down there, and I didn't want to meet him, not yet. I'd been watching him all evening.

When Hans walked into the ring I started sweating. Almost every time I saw him, I thought; I should have taken him in.

I'd clapped when Josh Hartley was boxing, so as not to arouse suspicion. Before the fight I'd stood in front of my bed with the expandable baton and pounded the pillow, but the feeling wasn't as satisfying as it had been with him.

I waited until the people had left the hall. I saw Hans down in the ring; he was leaning on the ropes staring at the plastic chairs, alone.

Opposite the Corn Exchange I stood in the entrance to a restaurant and waited for Hans. I was wearing a black coat with a dark hoodie underneath. No one going past noticed me.

The restaurant belonged to a TV chef with tattooed arms; it was full every evening, but now, just before midnight, it was closed. Many years ago, when I was a student here, this building housed an old library, with a domed reading room in the middle and bookshelves that were slightly curved to fit the library's rounded walls. I looked at the evening menu, which hung in a glass case on the wall. It offered "artisan bread" for four pounds and "our famous crab linguini" for thirteen pounds fifty.

This library was where I wrote my final dissertation. Back then I was just discovering the Dutch painters and was so obsessed with Rembrandt's *The Return of the Prodigal Son* that I applied to my college for a travel grant to fly to Leningrad, because I was desperate to see the original in the Hermitage.

It was the hands in the painting. I wanted to see the hands. The father embracing the son who had disappointed him and now knelt before him in rags, asking for forgiveness. The father's left hand was that of a man, strong, gripping the son's shoulder; the right hand was delicate, the hand of a woman.

When I saw the original I was startled because it was so big. The colors were warm. None of his other paintings express Rembrandt's faith in love quite like this. The father was able to forgive because he loved.

I'd always been too afraid to try and talk to Hans, to ask him for forgiveness.

Hans

The ringside doctor said that while my nose was this badly swollen he wouldn't be able to tell whether or not I would need an operation. He could reset the bone right away, but it would be painful and would damage more blood vessels. Charlotte was waiting outside the dressing room. I'd taken my time, had stayed in the ring till the hall was empty.

I took a long, cold shower, as the doctor had recommended, to help close the blood vessels. He'd said that on no account should I blow my nose; it would push the blood up into my eyes and everything would turn red. A typical boxer's story; I didn't believe it.

A light-blue, thick felt blazer was hanging in the dressing room. *Hans Stichler* was written on the hanger. The day after the coach announced the team we'd gone to the tailor to be measured. Later on, I sometimes wondered what happened to the blazers of boxers who lost. Only those who won their matches were allowed to wear the blue. I stroked the rough material. The light blue of Cambridge University was actually more green than blue. I'd have called it aquamarine if that didn't sound silly. I put my face against the fabric.

"You earned it."

Charlotte stood in the open doorway of the changing room. She wasn't smiling.

"I'd like to talk to you about earlier," she said. "It wasn't OK, the way you grabbed my wrist."

It took a while for this sentence to reach me. Blood was seeping through the paper in my nose and dripping onto the light blue blazer. It looked brown and ugly on the material.

"I don't understand."

"I swore to myself that no man would ever touch me again if I didn't want him to." She reached inside the blazer and stroked the material. "Such a cold color."

I remembered how she had slept on my elbow in Somerset. I went to put my hands on her shoulders, then drew back, because I was afraid.

"I don't know whether we belong together," she said.

"I'm sorry—I was just worried about you."

I stood there like that for a moment or two, then went into the bathroom to fetch some more paper for my nose. She tried not to make any noise as she walked out of the dressing room and down the stairs. She left my mother's necklace on top of my sports bag.

I stood in front of the mirror, took my nasal bone between my hands and pulled it straight. Then I turned off the light and left the dressing room.

*　*　*

Alex emerged from the darkness. Hands in her coat pockets, she stepped out of a doorway. She saw the blood running down my chin, took the scarf from her neck and gave it to me.

"You'll never get it out," I said.

She shrugged. I held the scarf under my nose. She stroked the sleeve of my blazer.

"Charlotte's already left," I said. Alex nodded.

She walked beside me without speaking and tentatively took my arm. I felt my muscles tense up. Until that day, the only physical contact between Alex and myself had been handshakes. Taking my arm was such a familiar, tender gesture that I wondered if something bad had happened.

In the shop windows we were walking past I saw suits with too-short jackets and sweatshirts with the slogan I ♥ CAMBRIDGE. I thought of Charlotte holding another man's hand.

"She'll come back, she's not like her father," said Alex.

"You know her father?"

"Sort of." She glanced at me. "You have to find out who did it, Hans."

"I know."

We walked silently, aimlessly, across the market square, then stopped for something to eat at the late-night kebab shop.

"Why didn't you send for me, back then?" I asked.

She sucked air through her teeth.

"I was too ill," she said. "There was a period when I wasn't myself."

"That's it?"

We were sitting side by side on a bench, not looking at each other. She spoke quietly.

"Do you know Goya's *Black Paintings*?"

"Alex."

"Yes."

"This is important to me. Please don't start talking about some paintings."

She leaned towards me. "Do you know Rembrandt's painting of the prodigal son?"

"What are you talking about?"

"Please—forgive me," she said.

When Alex put her thin arms around me I was so shocked that initially I recoiled as if she were trying to hit me. Her sharp collarbone dug into my chest. I wondered why her hug didn't feel warm, and that was when I realized I would never forgive her. She had come too late.

"I'm tired," I said.

"Hans, please . . ."

I got up and went home. An animal was leaping through the branches of a tree; a squirrel, I think. Squirrels are never afraid of falling.

In my room I hung the bandages on the door to dry, put on a white shirt and tied my bow tie. I could do it without looking now. I put on the new, light-blue blazer.

The other boxers were already at the Pitt Club, celebrating. They hugged me and talked about the fights. I drank vodka out of the trophy the team had won, too fast and too much, because I didn't want to think about Charlotte any more. Afterwards, at the bar, I knocked back four tequila slammers with lemon and salt. A woman stroked my new blazer. Another asked if I was the German boxer. Josh asked me if I wanted to do a line of coke. He'd used eye pencil to paint himself blue. I pointed to my broken nose and shook my head. He touched my blazer and said something like, "Safe jacket, right?" Josh knew everything that went on at the Club; he'd been at the university as long as Charlotte. I felt I could hardly bear any more of this.

A woman put two tequilas in my hands and unbuttoned my shirt. I let her do it. She sprinkled salt on the skin between my collarbone and my chest, licked it, drank the tequilas, and flung the slice of lemon onto the dance floor. The woman examined the cuts on my face and said she was studying medicine. She was like an insect.

I was partying in the club where my girlfriend had been assaulted, and chatting intimately with another woman. I was drinking and dancing with the men who might have done it.

There had been evenings at this club when I'd felt as if my real self were slowly dissolving and at some point only Hans Stichler would be left. That evening, though, I knew exactly who I was, and who I didn't want to be.

I left without saying goodbye and walked through the empty streets. For the first time I noticed that in Cambridge hardly anyone spat chewing gum on the ground. The pavement gleamed in the light from the streetlamps. The blue blazer, the shining cobbles, the neat grass in the college courts, the black gowns, the white pillars of the Pitt Club all combined to create and preserve the myth that made this place great. I remembered how much I'd wanted to belong; but tonight, when I was finally wearing the university colors, when I finally did belong, it disgusted me.

I blew my nose into a napkin I'd taken from the Club and dropped the bloody tissue on the ground. Walking back to college I was cold, and the felt blazer scratched my neck. I wished Billy were there and I could tell him the truth. That night I would have done. When I got back I went to the bathroom and looked in the mirror. My eyes were red.

Hans

The first meeting with the Butterflies took place in Josh's kitchen. He was pacing up and down in front of the cooker in a cotton apron he'd knotted over his stomach, frying prawns in olive oil and garlic. He took the prawns out of the oil, let them drain onto a paper towel, and arranged them on the plates; he chopped coriander and chili, scattered them over the prawns and sprinkled them with coarse sea salt.

"Squeeze the lime juice on yourselves, my young whip-persnappers," he said.

With me at the table sat four former boxers, all of whom I knew from the Club. They'd been on the team in recent years and were still at the university. All of them had greeted me with a hug. Beside me sat the man who had beaten Billy up in the Pitt Club at the start of the year.

Any one of them could be a rapist. Underneath the table I dug my fingernails into the wood until the nail on my right index finger snapped.

At the start of the summer term I'd found in my pigeon-hole an envelope with the butterfly seal and an invitation to this dinner at Josh's.

The five men talked about the boxing match, laughing when one of them imitated Magic Mike. Josh said something or other about blue African vampire shrimps. I'd come here expecting something sinister, and now I was sitting with five guys drinking white wine in a fancy kitchen. I found it unbearable to be laughing with them.

Josh said the Butterflies were a club of young men who swore always to stand by one another. All members had to fulfill certain criteria, the details of which were complicated, but they all had to be Pitt Club members who had won a box-ing match against Oxford.

The Butterflies had been around for as long as anyone could remember. Josh said all this in a conversational tone, but then his expression grew serious.

"No one on the outside knows about us," he said, and squeezed my arm.

A few days ago someone had slid a copy of Charlotte's doctor's report under my door. I'd read the report again, and now, as I watched the prawns slowly turn red in Josh's frying pan, dancing in the hot oil, all I could think about were Charlotte's tears. The last thing I felt like doing was eating.

Josh refilled our glasses with Chablis. He said the Butterflies would accept me as one of their number. There were always five active members, he said, and Paul—he put his hand on one man's shoulder—was graduating this year, so a place would soon be free. The initiation ritual was old and parts of it were a bit—Josh gazed out of the window—a bit unconventional. The other boys smirked. Josh reached for the little terracotta garden gnome on his windowsill and tossed it in the air; the gnome described a single somersault and fell back into his hand.

"I don't think anyone's ever regretted it," he said.

I looked around the group. "How do you know I want to join?"

"Everyone wants to join," said Josh.

I nodded.

"Are you with us, my friend?" Josh asked.

For a moment I hesitated, but no one said anything; I don't suppose they noticed.

"Sure," I said. A single word that cost me everything I had.

"Boom," said Josh.

I heard the chink of crystal. One of the boys said I should

think carefully about whether I planned to go on spending time with Billy—the man must surely have lice. Another asked me whether I was interested in doing an internship that summer at a private bank in Zurich; he knew someone there, and it would be perfect for me, being fluent in German.

"More prawns?" asked Josh.

"They're good," I said.

I ate another two. The prawns tasted of salt and the sea. All of you are going to pay, I thought.

Back in my room I sat at my desk and took a fresh notebook off the shelf. I'd briefly considered writing on the computer, but that didn't seem right. For the first time in years I wrote a diary entry. The first sentence was: *Her name is Charlotte.*

I had forgotten how good writing made me feel. My pen glided over the lines. It was getting light outside when I closed the notebook. I opened a window. I wouldn't get any sleep tonight. The air smelled of spring and a new day.

Josh

Face masks are a good idea, for men, too, for the following reasons. They remove makeup, rejuvenate the complexion, moisturize, and they make the skin more elastic, less likely to split, which of course is particularly important for boxers.

I was sitting on my own in the kitchen as day began to break, waiting for my chamomile and jojoba cleansing mask to take effect. The dirty dishes and a plate of prawn carcasses were piled up in front of me. The lads had stayed late. I wondered why Stichler had hesitated for a moment, and why he'd left so early. Mates don't leave early, they stay till the end. What was the matter? I'd been a Butterfly for four years. No one had ever hesitated.

To set my mind at ease I thought about all the women I'd shagged. Whenever I went through the list I always got stuck on the blonde girl the lads had invited a few years earlier. I wasn't sure whether she belonged on the list or not. I remembered the evening she walked into the Club. She had this warmth about her.

I barely remembered the end of it, though. I'd only been a Butterfly for a couple of months at the time. The party got a bit too crazy: too much Chartreuse, plus three-and-a-half lines of coke to clear my head, which of course did not have the desired effect. Afterwards: memory fucked.

Memory one: Sitting on the closed lid of the toilet at the Club, bleeding from both nostrils and feeling like the king of the world. That didn't explain the dried blood I washed off my thighs the next morning, though. I still remember scraping it off and sniffing it. It didn't smell of woman.

I still don't know what the others did with her. I bet it makes for a strong story, possibly too big a one to tell.

Memory two: The scent of a woman, mixed with the smell of peppermints. *La nuit tous les chats sont gris.* Such a cool saying.

Maybe I should have explained to Stichler who we really were. The boxing, the connections, none of that was important. The Butterflies were friends. That sounds gay, but it's what counts. Friendship was the reason we existed. It was why we did everything together, good stuff and bad. It meant far more than all the other crap: the blue blazer, the birds, the money, the contacts. It was all about friendship. I was sure Stichler would understand.

I put the plates in the sink for the cleaning woman. I always felt a bit sorry for her because of her rank job, and because she had shit for brains and came from Poland.

I briefly considered boiling up the prawn carcasses into a stock, but I was too tired. I washed my face in the kitchen sink, went into the bedroom and stood in front of the mirrored wardrobe. I removed my clothes until I stood naked in front of the mirror, and took a look at myself as God made me. When I flicked off the light switch with my big toe, I was smiling.

Hans

A few weeks later, Billy and I were sitting on the edge of the fountain in the market square eating soft buttered rolls filled with chips.

"Chip butties are the best fucking thing the English ever invented, apart from football," said Billy.

It was the afternoon before my Butterflies initiation ritual. I assumed I'd be drinking a lot of alcohol. There was a party at the Pitt Club that evening. I'd told Billy I'd like to go and get something to eat with him beforehand; I needed to line my stomach. We'd hardly seen each other since the fight. Billy said there were two things you had to think about when going on a bender: carbohydrates and fat.

"The best thing to do is to drink a bit of olive oil beforehand."

He took two brown balls wrapped in greaseproof paper out of his rucksack.

"Scotch eggs," he said.

I ate them, holding my breath. They were a bit like burgers, as big as his fist, with a hard-boiled egg in the middle. Billy licked his fingers.

"I know I've been weird these last few weeks," I said. "I'll explain it all to you one day."

"Me too," said Billy.

Before we said goodbye, he took a small stone out of his rucksack and gave it to me. It was shiny and looked as if someone had turned it over and over in their pocket.

"It'll bring you luck," said Billy.

I looked at this young, longhaired man who, for no apparent reason, had come up and talked to me a few months ago. Perhaps those were the best kind of meetings. I held out my hand.

"Thanks," I said.

Billy clasped my hand and shook it.

Charlotte

After my night at the Pitt Club I walked past the pigeonholes in my college almost every day for three years, looking for an envelope with a yellow butterfly seal. I was relieved that I never found one.

Then a few months before Hans came up to Cambridge I saw a yellow envelope in another female student's pigeonhole. I glanced out of the window to see if anyone was watching and removed the envelope. On the back I saw a yellow wax seal stamped with a butterfly. I slipped the letter into my pocket.

Back in my room I started shaking. I opened the bottom left-hand drawer of my desk, pushed aside some papers and the doctor's report and took out the letter I'd received three years earlier. The seals were identical. I opened the new envelope with a bread knife. The handwriting on this invitation was different, but the words were the same.

My blood ran cold. I grabbed a padded jacket, left the room and wandered round Cambridge for a while like a lost soul. As I found myself walking towards the station, I considered taking the next train to London and never coming back. Perhaps I could start a new life. But I knew this was the only life there was.

Apart from my friend and the hospital doctors, I hadn't told anyone about that night. My friend had asked me so many times to file a complaint against a person or persons unknown that we were both relieved when she graduated and moved to Cape Town.

I'd requested a copy of the examination report. The doctors had informed the police, and a few weeks later I'd received a letter asking me to come to the police station and make a statement. I went and told them it had been a misunderstanding. I'd slept with a hammer under my pillow ever since.

I'd never gone back to the Pitt Club, and when Father asked if I wanted to accompany him to their Alumni Ball I declined, though there was no way he could have known why.

I took my phone out of my bag and wrote an e-mail to Alex.

Dear Alex,

I'd like to make an appointment with you. It's not about my PhD, it's a private matter and it's important. When would you have time? It's urgent. I need to see you today, please.

All the best,

Charlotte

Alex

When we interview students as part of the selection process, we like to ask them questions to which there is no answer. What is time? Do we have an obligation to save strangers? And a question that's become rather unfashionable these days, but of all the mean questions it's still my favorite: Is it right to kill one person to save a hundred?

The applicants who've been educated at expensive boarding schools talk about utilitarianism and Peter Singer. One of them once managed to find a way of linking the question to the issue of global hunger. The clever applicants talk about Kant and human dignity, which is supposedly violated if you use a person as a means to an end.

I don't believe in God, as Kant did. I don't believe people are unique in that they have something some philosophers call "dignity," and that this something sets us apart from beasts.

What sets us apart from apes is that we have the capacity to exact revenge. Not just to bite back; to exercise patience, conceive a plan, enact this plan, and find satisfaction in it when it succeeds.

I liked Charlotte. She was a good girl and a talented art historian.

Charlotte

"What can I do for you, Charlotte?" asked Alex, the day I found the letter. She was sitting on the edge of her desk in jeans and a white T-shirt, and she looked great.

"Before I tell you, please—no lectures about why I didn't say anything before," I said.

"That doesn't sound good," said Alex.

I took the letter out of my pocket, put it on the table, and told her everything.

She took the new envelope, stroked her index finger across the seal, and closed her eyes. She sat like that for a few seconds, then looked at me.

"When you were at the hospital, did they do all the usual tests for someone in your situation?"

I didn't know what tests were usually done on someone who'd been raped, but I said yes.

"Why have you come to me?"

I'd practiced my speech in front of the mirror in my room four times, because I was afraid I might burst into tears. Now this question. Why had I come to Alex? The real reason was that she was a woman. And because I knew she traveled to Iraq during the war to examine a long-lost Picasso and verify its authenticity. The painting was called *The Naked Woman*. Alex drove through the desert in an armored Humvee to reach it. She was also the one who'd persuaded me to stay on at Cambridge after my undergraduate degree. I liked her because she didn't wear tweed jackets, she drank beer, she was a feminist, and she had the reputation of being one of the brightest women in the country. After graduation I'd thought about where I wanted to work. My friends opted for management consultancy, banking; one went to MI6. I saw no reason why I should work in a bank. Alex told me: *Do a PhD. I don't usually supervise PhD students, but I'll supervise you.*

Father was against it. He begged me to go and get a job. Even then, though, I already wanted to curate exhibitions, and I knew I stood a much better chance of getting a job in a museum if I had a PhD. I could have asked Father to help me, but I thought it was wrong to use connections in order to get a position.

No other university would have provided the level of supervision I had at Cambridge. I felt I was strong because I'd stayed. I hadn't run away. But every time I walked past the white pillars of the Pitt Club my heart started racing.

"Why have you come to me?" Alex asked again.

"Because you're the vice-rector. You've known this place for forty years; I thought you might be able to help. And because I trust you."

"You don't want to go to the police because you don't want to have to testify?"

"I'd even make a statement."

"But you want to avoid a messy trial."

I nodded.

"Everything would be dragged up again and made public," said Alex.

She sat opposite me, calm and focused. I'd come to the right person.

"What do you want?"

I felt the blood rush to my face. What did I want? That was what this was about. I felt as if I were sitting an exam.

"No idea. Justice. I don't know. I don't want it ever to happen again."

She stared at me. I didn't blink.

"Justice," she said.

"Yes . . . I mean . . . I hope that's possible."

What she said next made me shiver. She spoke so quietly I could barely understand, and I pretended I hadn't heard her.

"You don't want justice, Charlotte."

Hans

At nine p.m. there was a knock on my door. I was wearing the new dinner jacket. At the first fitting Angus Farewell had said it shone like ivory black. Billy's little stone was in my trouser pocket. I quickly reached up to the shelf, took down a miniature bottle of olive oil and drank the lot just before Josh and the four Butterflies entered my room. They were early. One undid my bow tie, took it from my neck and threw it in the bin. He reached into his inside jacket pocket, took out another tie in the Pitt Club colors and dangled it in front of my nose, then turned it over so I could see the outline of a little yellow butterfly on the inside, embroidered onto the silk. Once the tie was fastened the butterfly was hidden.

On the way to the Pitt Club Josh said that tonight we were celebrating the Feast of the Holy Trinity. For women, that meant they could only wear three items of clothing. Shoes and earrings counted as items of clothing.

Almost all the women at the Club were barefoot. One was wearing a bikini, another was in a hooded leotard with rabbit ears, one was wearing a long black dress and two earrings. The men were in dinner jackets. Everyone was observing the rules. What was actually wrong with these women?

The Butterflies accompanied me to the bar. They each bought me a drink that I had to down in one. I'd got to know a lot of new drinks that year—Cape Codders, Rob Roys, Yellow Jackets—all of which tasted predominantly of alcohol.

The Butterflies dragged me onto the dance floor, where I jumped up and down a bit and pretended I was having fun. It smelled of expensive women's perfume and tequila. I lost all sense of time. At some point I went outside and sat down on the curb; for a moment I was afraid Charlotte might show up. Josh sat down beside me and put his arm around my shoulders. He often touched me. He talked about how he might extend his PhD so he could party and box for a few more years.

Next to us two girls were smoking a joint.

"Excuse me, ladies, could you do that somewhere else?" said Josh.

The Pitt Club began to empty around three a.m. Josh was leaning against a bookshelf beside me. He pointed to a girl in the crowd in a tight gold catsuit that clung to every inch of her body. She was laughing and dancing with her friends. I wondered what other items of clothing she had on.

"That's ours," said Josh.

I looked past the girl at the wood-paneled wall and pictured the forest from which the wood had come. How I would have liked to have been in that forest.

"Go get some more fresh air, brother, you look kind of battered. We're in the lounge behind the bar, OK?" said Josh.

I nodded and left the room. At the top of the staircase I paused, turned, and watched Josh go up to the girl in the gold catsuit and put his arm around her. He talked to her for a bit and pulled her over to the bar. One of the other Butterflies tapped her on the shoulder. As she turned, Josh took a little plastic bottle out of his pocket and tipped a clear liquid into her glass. He looked at the other Butterfly and gave him a thumbs-up. He kissed the girl on the cheek and whispered something in her ear. The little plastic bottle was dropped on the floor.

The DJ played "Summer of '69," then turned the music down. Waiters and security guards passed through the Club asking the guests to go home. Josh took the girl in the gold catsuit by the hand and led her through a door behind the bar. She was steadying herself on the wall, and her knees buckled slightly with every step.

I locked myself in a toilet cubicle because I needed a moment to compose myself, whatever that meant.

When I went back into the room it was empty apart from the waiters. I went to the bar, wrapped the little bottle Josh had dropped in a napkin, and put it in the silk-lined pocket of my dinner jacket. Then I opened the door behind the bar.

One of the men pushed the door shut. The room was about fifty square meters, with a billiard table in the middle. A glass case was hung at the vanishing point at the other end of the room, with a ceiling lamp angled at the case. Close up, I saw that it contained a yellow butterfly: ORNITHOPTERA GOLIATH, NEW GUINEA was written underneath. I touched the glass with the back of my hand.

Whatever the girl had drunk, it had worked fast. She started licking Josh all over his face. "Hold me," she kept saying. "Hold me." She was stroking herself. Her hands slid over the golden fabric, over her breasts, her belly, her crotch, her thighs. I could barely look at her. She was pure libido.

Josh pushed her onto a sofa and she made no attempt to get up. The men formed a circle, each putting their arms around their neighbors' shoulders, and took me into their midst. I closed my eyes, not knowing what else to do.

"Repeat after us," said Josh.

He recited an old-fashioned English oath, which I repeated. Later, I recalled one sentence in particular: "I was a caterpillar; the Club has given me wings."

The girl on the sofa started mewing. Josh went over to her, picked her up, carried her across the room, and laid her on the billiard table. I stood in front of her. She gazed at me; her eyes were all pupil. She spread her legs and wrapped them around my back.

"You're so serious," she said.

"What's your name?"

"Whatever you like."

"What's your name?"

"Lucia."

Josh sat on the table beside the girl, dangling his feet. Then he grabbed the material over her crotch and ripped the golden catsuit from her body. She was wearing knickers with little cherries printed on them. I stood between the girl's legs, not looking at her as she writhed before me on the table. I could feel the heat coming off her. She grabbed my neck with both hands and pulled me down. Her tongue was on my face and in my mouth. She wanted it; at that moment, she wanted it.

I hated the Club, but I was part of it now. I was someone.

Her thighs pressed against something in my trouser pocket. The stone. I slid my hand into the pocket and my fingers touched its smooth, cool surface. Abruptly I raised my head and stared at the wall again.

I remembered.

I knew where I'd seen that yellow butterfly before.

I pushed myself up, reached behind my back, and un-locked the girl's legs. My hands rested briefly on her feet. Josh stroked my hair.

"In the rainforest, some butterflies live by drinking tears. Beautiful, isn't it?" he said, so quietly I could hardly hear him.

At Cambridge I'd learned how many great things hu-mans are capable of. They can establish the basis of formal logic, calculate the speed of light, and discover anti-malaria medicine. But I'd also learned at Cambridge what humans are at heart: predators.

I sank onto one of the sofas and watched Josh move in front of the girl and undo his trousers. She was breathing heavily. "Thank you," she murmured.

I thought of Charlotte and her scars. Perhaps she had lain on this very table. I was fulfilling my mission by incriminating myself. There was no clean way out of this. It hadn't been clean since Alex had told me that sometimes it was right to deceive people. The girl would be raped, I would testify against Josh in court, and he would receive his punishment. I would have to allow this crime to take place, otherwise the Butterflies would just keep doing it to other women. Perhaps that was why old people walked with a stoop, bowed down by the weight of deci-sions which may have been right but still felt wrong.

Right or wrong, it seemed to me that there were no clear answers any more. Perhaps everything really was gray.

The coach had once told me that, after years in the gym, years of fighting, some boxers reach a state where you can no longer knock them out. Even if they take a perfect upper cut to the chin and their brain shuts down for a moment to protect itself against injury, their subconscious carries on boxing. They don't fall down. In this state they do things they don't remember; but sometimes it's precisely those seconds that save them.

My movements were faster than I thought they would be. Josh was standing in front of the girl with his trousers down. He smiled when I pushed his hip aside; he was expecting me to do something else. The girl was very thin; I could hardly feel the weight of her as I pushed her legs together and lifted her off the table. I opened the door, into the front room and down the stairs, carrying the girl in my arms. The Butterflies' shouts weren't important now. I was surprised no one followed me. Perhaps Alex would be angry, perhaps I was in the process of ruining everything I'd worked for over the best part of a year, but there was no "perhaps" any more. There was no gray. I had made my decision.

I asked the girl which college she was in.

"Caius. St Michael's Court," she said, eyes closed.

She snuggled up to me and fell asleep in my arms. After a few minutes of carrying her through the streets my biceps started to ache and I had to put her down to give them a rest, but she still didn't open her eyes, just stood there propped against me. Her college porter just winked when I asked him the way to her room.

She shared a set with another female student. It was four in the morning when I knocked. After a minute or two the door was opened by a young woman in a dressing gown. "Lucia" was all she said.

"Sit by her bed and keep an eye on her," I said. "She's taken some kind of drug and I don't know how she's going to react."

I carried the girl into her room and put her to bed. Then I left before her roommate could ask me any questions. My arms were stiff and aching.

The sun would soon be up. Back in my room I picked up my passport and a credit card and took the train to the airport. I booked a flight to Hanover on my mobile phone; the flight was expensive, but I didn't care.

When I landed in Germany there was a train straight from the airport to the village where I grew up. It was one of the old trains, with soft upholstery and windows you could pull down. I was still wearing my dinner jacket, but I'd taken off the bow tie. The wind blew in my face as we sped along.

I got out at my home village and walked the four kilometers into the forest. At the end there was an avenue of chestnut trees; there were no cars at this time of day and I walked in the middle of the road, the asphalt crunching beneath my leather soles. I hadn't been back here since my parents died.

The house in the forest had been renovated. There was a gleaming 4×4 in the drive. The new owners had laid the front to lawn and reroofed the house with black tiles. Before, the tiles were red and covered with moss. I knocked on the door. A blonde girl opened it; she was about seven years old and had a gap in her teeth.

I was startled by how young her mother was. She looked younger than me. I told her I used to live in the house and happened to be in the area. She said she'd heard about us from the previous owners; she was sorry about the business with my parents.

"Is the cherry tree still there?" I asked.

"The one out the back?" asked the woman.

I walked around the house. I didn't want to go in, so as not to destroy my memories of it, but she didn't invite me in, either.

It was late May. I could hear bees. The cherry tree was at least three meters high and covered in delicate pink blossoms. A swing hung from one of the branches. The blonde girl was hiding behind the corner of the house; she reminded me of Charlotte in the photo in Somerset. I placed one hand on the trunk of the tree. The woman brought me a pale tea; she said she made it from the cherry blossom, it was good for the energy flow. The tea tasted of hot water.

I leaned my back against the tree and beckoned to the girl. She laughed. I gave her Billy's stone and closed her fingers over it.

The woman came running over. "Get your hands off my daughter!" Her voice was high and metallic.

I left without looking back. I walked to the station and knew I would never return.

Hans

On the table in Alex's office stood three cups of tea, but no one was drinking. Charlotte was wearing a tracksuit; she was pale and her hair looked unwashed. I wanted to put my arms around her but didn't dare, because Alex was standing by the window.

I told them about the girl in the gold catsuit and put the little plastic bottle on the table.

"Have you touched it?" asked Alex.

"No, the fingerprints should still be on it."

Tears were running down Charlotte's cheeks.

"Probably liquid ecstasy," said Alex. She explained that this was a sexual stimulant, and often had the effect of erasing your memory. Alex said she would have the bottle analyzed in a lab, and then she wanted to find the girl in the gold catsuit.

"No judge will condemn anyone on account of a fingerprint and a crime that wasn't committed," I said.

"We don't need a judge," said Alex. "I know the editor-in-chief of the biggest newspaper in the country. That's enough."

Charlotte picked up her tea. The china cup clattered on the saucer.

"It'll be over soon," said Alex. I wasn't sure who she was talking to.

"One more thing, Hans, and then we've got it all. I need a list with the names of all the Butterflies, past and present."

I looked out of the window.

"Where am I supposed to get that from?" I asked; and as I did so I realized the deception, the betrayal, would be total. I grabbed my coat from the stand and left. Charlotte caught up with me on the stairs.

"I'm sorry about the thing with your arm," I said.

"My fault," said Charlotte.

She stopped on the step above me and put her arms around my neck. I could smell her tears. I didn't know whether I was supporting her or she me.

"It's all my fault," she said.

"Nothing's your fault," I said.

I looked out of the staircase window and saw a couple of students going into the library. I envied them. Charlotte leaned her head on my shoulder. It was a small movement.

As soon as I was alone I called Angus Farewell at his office.

"It's Hans."

"Hans, good to hear from you. Is there something the matter with Charlotte?"

"She's fine. I just wanted to ask if I could drop in to see you in London. In passing."

I listened to my voice and wondered whether it sounded different when I was lying.

Two days later, Farewell picked me up in the car from King's Cross Station. It would only have been a short journey to Chelsea by Underground and bus, but he'd said it was far too complicated.

"How's Charlie?" he asked when we got to a traffic light.

"Fine. She's on the last few pages of her thesis."

We were sitting in the Jaguar Charlotte and I had driven to Somerset a couple of months earlier. It felt like a long time ago. I ran my hand over the old leather of the seat.

The journey took quite a while; it was Friday, rush hour traffic. Farewell parked the car on the gravel drive in front of the house. He said we could go out onto the terrace; Joyce would make us some sandwiches. The lawn had been freshly mown. I'd always loved that smell. We sat on chairs made of tropical wood.

"So, what can I do for you?" Farewell asked.

"I just wanted to see you again." My heart was pounding.

I pulled the new bow tie out of my trouser pocket. It was a bit crumpled, and for a moment I was slightly embarrassed. I turned it over until I found the yellow butterfly. Farewell took the tie from me and ran the silk through his hands.

"A young Butterfly," he said. His face betrayed no emotion.

Joyce brought a silver tray with cucumber sandwiches and asked us what we would like to drink.

"Just sparkling water," said Farewell. I nodded. Neither of us ate anything.

"I thought you'd be pleased," I said.

Farewell handed back the tie.

"I am. I'm pleased for you. But I've been hearing some worrying stories. We were wild too, forty years ago, but what I heard sounded . . . different."

There was singing coming from the kitchen; it distracted me. Farewell took a deep breath.

"We had our fun as well, but it was more the girls who made us do it. It was a sort of game among the women—bagging one of us, getting us into bed."

For the sake of something to do, I took a cucumber sandwich from the tray. I wanted to get away from here, away from this man.

Farewell grabbed my arm. "Have you done something to a girl, Hans?" he asked.

My chin trembled for a second. This was crazy; I didn't know what to believe any more. I shook my head. Farewell nodded.

"Some men go a bit peculiar when they're accepted as one of us," he said. "The power . . . some men can't deal with it. Being powerful means having to take responsibility. Do you understand?"

"I think so," I said.

"It's like boxing. We don't just lash out if someone gives us a nasty look in the pub. There are some things you just don't do."

The cucumber sandwich had stuck in my throat; I had to wash it down with sparkling water. Farewell said he would raise the subject at the next meeting of the Club. Students weren't allowed to come to these meetings until after they had graduated, so perhaps they weren't aware of who exactly was in the Club and how many people's reputations would be damaged were they to be associated with assaults on young women. He said the word "assaults" very quietly.

"Who exactly *is* in the Club?" I asked, trying and failing to sound casual.

"I've already told you: important people whose reputations could be damaged if their names were to be made public. But seeing as you're family, so to speak . . ."

He named a few names. I could see how pleased he was with himself. Some of them I knew, some I'd never heard of. How easy it was to deceive a person.

I finished my sparkling water, excused myself, went to one of the bathrooms on the ground floor and typed the names into my phone. I wasn't able to remember them all. Before I left the bathroom I ran my hand over one of the gold taps, for the last time.

Farewell talked a bit longer, about boxing, and said I absolutely must spar a few rounds with him. I said that my nose hadn't yet fully healed; I would come back after the summer vacation.

The cucumber sandwiches were drying up at the edges. Farewell offered to drive me to the station, but I insisted on taking the Underground. We shook hands and said goodbye.

"Give Charlie a kiss from me," he said, and smiled.

I nodded, blushing slightly. As I was walking up the drive Farewell opened the door again.

"How's the dinner jacket?" he called across the forecourt.

"Wonderful," I called back. "Wonderfully soft, thank you."

Angus

Early morning, no sun, a day that began like any other. I drove to the office. I hadn't slept much the past two nights, but I'd got used to that since my wife died. It was now more worrying if I slept a lot; that made me feel old. The previous evening I had lain awake for a long time thinking about Stichler and the Butterflies. He'd seemed nervous, and I couldn't explain to myself why that might have been. Were he and Charlotte a couple?

At the office I had a telephone conference with my colleagues in Sydney. Increasing yields; everything was fine. In fact, everything was always fine: I'd grown used to it. I was browsing the theatre listings on my laptop when the phone rang. One of my secretaries told me an Alexandra Birk was downstairs in reception.

There are calls I dread receiving, which is why I often run through them in my mind. The policeman who calls to tell me Charlotte has been in a car crash. The doctor who calls and tells me I have blood cancer. I hadn't dreaded this call from my secretary, but when it came I knew that I should have done.

I closed my eyes for a moment.

"Alexandra," I said.

"May I show her up?" asked the secretary.

"No," I said quickly.

For a moment there was silence on the line. The secretary cleared her throat. "Miss Birk says I should tell you it's about the butterflies." She giggled as if it were funny. Still I didn't speak.

Finally I said, "Show her up, please."

The first time we spoke to each other was at a party at St. John's College, forty years ago. We danced a bit, I remember it clearly. She wrote me long letters; I found her attractive and a little bit strange. She wore her hair short. She came to the boxing gym a few times and wanted to train. We even sparred once. She put a lot of effort into it; she had no technique, but I let her hit me a couple of times. She punched so hard and so wildly I had to put her in a clinch. She bit my ear and whispered, "Hitting you turns me on."

I slept with her on the billiard table in the back room of the Pitt Club. I hadn't planned to, but, drunk and stoned as I was, I was happy to let her drag me off the dance floor.

She had a muscular body and no pubic hair, which seemed exotic to me at the time. The sex was good. We kissed for a long time, and then I laid her on the table. When I took off her trousers she started hitting me. I hesitated for a moment, because I didn't know whether she was resisting or whether, for her, that was part of the fun; but she didn't say anything, just looked at me. She hit me, then she kissed me, and with that it was clear. She was an animal, but she turned me on. Afterwards my lip was bleeding and I was still aroused.

The next day my bow tie was missing, and I went round to knock on Alexandra's door because I wanted to ask her if she had it. I think I smiled at her, because we both knew what had happened the previous night; there was a red mark over my left cheekbone. I had a headache, and when I saw her standing in the doorway in a baggy white T-shirt that came down to her thighs I wondered whether I really ought to go in. I asked her to return the bow tie. To my surprise she started crying; she kept saying, "You shouldn't have done that." I decided there and then that this woman was too unhinged for me, however good the sex had been. I was sure I'd be able to calm her down. When I left I gave her a kiss on the forehead, and as she didn't react it seemed to me everything was OK. I would keep out of her way in future. I walked back to my room, changed my clothes, and went to Ryder & Amies to remove the swatch from the book.

After that, when I stood at the window of my room in the evenings, I would often see Alexandra lurking in the college library, in one of the high-ceilinged rooms on an upper floor, staring out at me. I threw her letters in the bin without reading them, and after university I forgot her.

Many years later the nighttime phone calls began. The caller never spoke, and if my wife answered they immediately hung up. If I answered, they stayed on the line. I knew it was Alexandra; I thought I recognized her breathing, but I couldn't say that to a policeman without sounding ridiculous. One day I saw her in Charlotte's kindergarten, standing there talking to her. Another time she walked through my garden, looking in at the windows. At that point the court issued a restraining order banning her from coming within a five-hundred-meter radius of my person. The anti-stalking legislation was only a few months old at the time, and I had to make a lot of phone calls to keep my case out of the papers. Naturally I made sure Charlotte and my wife didn't know about it.

I heard nothing more of Alexandra until Charlotte told me who she wanted to supervise her PhD. I asked her not to do it, I begged her, but sometimes Charlotte can be as stubborn as her mother. I called Alexandra and told her she couldn't do this, but she replied matter-of-factly that Charlotte had nothing to do with the past. I was reassured. I hadn't seen or spoken to Alexandra since.

A few months ago I got a call in the middle of the night. No one spoke; all I heard was that familiar, uneasy breathing.

Alexandra kept her eyes lowered as she entered my office. Her nails were freshly manicured, her makeup understated. I was irritated to find myself thinking that she was still a beautiful woman, though perhaps a little too thin.

"Alexandra," I said, "I thought we'd agreed that you would get on and live your own life."

"Angus."

She just said my name, as if it were a spell or curse—I couldn't interpret her tone—and gazed at me for several seconds. When she spoke again it was calmly, though it must have been a considerable effort. Her left eyelid flickered with every syllable.

"I know all about the Butterflies. I know that you abuse young women. Just like you abused me back then."

I looked at the clock on the wall behind her. I had a telephone conference with my colleagues in New York in a quarter of an hour. I had to get her out of my office before then. I could manage that.

"I didn't abuse you."

"You shouldn't have done what you did."

"You kissed me, Alexandra."

I sat on my desk. I'd been a businessman for too long to show any weakness when confronted. She had seen a yellow embroidered butterfly on my bow tie, many years ago. That was all.

"Do you hear voices?" I asked.

She didn't answer, and for the first time she looked uncomfortable.

"You know nothing, Alexandra, and no one will believe you. You're not well."

She walked right up to me and whispered the names in my ear. The names of the most powerful Butterflies. CEOs, politicians, bankers. She took her time. Then she said the last name. Mine.

I heard her breathing. My face grew hot. She stood in front of me and nodded.

"You can't do anything," I said.

"Oh, I can do a great deal." She turned and headed for the door.

"What do you want?" I shouted. The walls were thick, opaque glass, but I was sure my secretaries could hear me. I had never shouted in my office before.

"Do you believe in chaos theory?" Alexandra asked quietly.

"What are you talking about? You're completely insane."

"It suggests that the flap of a butterfly's wings in Brazil can cause a tornado in Texas."

"What's that got to do with me?"

Her body was rigid with tension.

"I am that butterfly."

"What is it you want?" I asked again, more quietly this time.

She smiled and left the room.

I sat down with my back to the window and looked around my office: glass, steel, a cherrywood table. I was sixty-one years old and I had achieved everything I wanted to achieve in life. I went out to speak to my executive secretary; as a rule I called her from my desk. She looked worried when I asked her to cancel all my appointments in the coming days; there was something I needed to deal with. I went downstairs in the lift and took the Underground to King's Cross. Standing in the train I clung on to a grubby pole; it was crowded and hot, and someone was eating noodles from a cardboard box; the whole compartment stank of it. I tried to convince myself that things weren't all that bad, and as I did so I knew that it was a lie. Behind me a child was sneezing.

Alex

I walked aimlessly through the streets. Angus had seemed genuinely surprised. At first he had inspected me as if to see how much I'd changed. There was nothing of that look left by the end. I would have liked to have stayed longer, just looking at his face.

Angus, I expect you're familiar with Gentileschi's *Judith and Holofernes*. After all, it befits men of your status to know a little bit about art. Gentileschi was a woman, by the way, in case you didn't know that. What I'm sure you don't know is that the painting isn't about the Old Testament story; it's about the artist herself. Artemisia Gentileschi was raped by one of her teachers when she was nineteen. He took her virginity, and during the trial that should have brought her rapist to justice she was humiliated a second time when the judges put thumbscrews on her and conducted a public examination to check her hymen. The painting shows the moment when Judith puts a dagger to Holofernes's throat and starts to cut off his head. It is possibly the most beautiful instance of revenge that has ever been immortalized in a painting; the expression of power and the depth of color are unparalleled, and I think it's no coincidence that this picture was painted by a woman. Wouldn't you agree, Angus?

I remember the first time he spoke to me, forty years ago, as if it were yesterday. He asked me where I'd gone to school and acted as if it didn't matter that I'd come from a Northern comprehensive. I liked the way he danced. I went to boxing training. It turned me on.

When I pulled him into the back room of the Pitt Club that night, I just wanted to kiss him. We kissed for a long time; it was nice. He took off my trousers. I didn't want that, so I hit him as hard as I could. He was too strong. I wanted to scream in his face and call for help, but I was so frightened I couldn't make a sound. I couldn't scream, so I hit him in the face and on the mouth. He took my wrists, twisted my arms behind my back, and the more I tried to defend myself the tighter and more painful it got. At some point I gave up and just waited for it to be over. It took a long time. He bit the back of my neck; I concentrated on that to distract myself from the pain in my abdomen. I felt his saliva on my neck. I was afraid he might kill me, so I started kissing him again. I hoped I would pass out, but I didn't, so I stared at the butterfly on the wall the whole time. I thought I must be rupturing inside. When he'd finished he fell asleep on a sofa. I took his bow tie, the tie with the embroidered butterfly. I had no ulterior motive.

The following day he came to my room. I don't remember why I opened the door to him. When he said goodbye he kissed me on the forehead, and I was so scared he might force himself on me again that I didn't dare move.

I wrote him letters asking him why he'd done it. I kept watch on him; I wanted him to know I wouldn't forget it. It didn't occur to me to go to the police. I felt guilty; I'd sent out the wrong signals. Years later a therapist told me that abuse takes many forms and that victims often feel guilty. Only then did it become clear to me that it was all his fault.

After that, the nightmares began. His mouth on my neck again. I clawed at him in my sleep and tried to scratch this man off my skin. On one of those nights, waking to a pillow flecked with blood, I called him for the first time. I knew that eventually the day would come when I would find some peace of mind.

When I saw Charlotte's name on the list of applicants, I didn't yet have a plan, just a satisfying feeling of getting closer to my goal. It was a mystery to me how a man like that could have such a wonderful daughter. She was everything he was not, and she deserved to know the truth.

I wanted him to feel what I had felt. The feeling of being an object. That was all. He should feel what it meant no longer to have any control over your own life.

I had the urge to run. I felt strong. I was fifty-nine years old, young enough to run another race this year. I still have a couple of marathons left in me. I dodged the bankers, the men emerging from skyscrapers, heading off to lunch. I darted past the gray suits. I speeded up; at some point I started sprinting. The heels of my shoes were too high, but I didn't care. Perhaps it was coincidence, everything coming together like this in the end; but I know that in reality there's no such thing as coincidence. I ran as if I were running for my life, breathing fast, sucking oxygen into my lungs. I wanted to keep on running and seeing the men make way for me.

Angus

The walk from the station into town was a short one, past cafés, colleges, people laughing as if nothing had happened. I didn't look at them.

I tried to call Charlotte; the phone rang to empty air. When she moved into her flat she had given me a key, just in case.

I rang her doorbell. No one answered, so I let myself in. "Hello? Charlie?"

Items of clothing on the floor, a few open drawers. I went over to her desk; I was afraid Alexandra might have written to her, or told her something. People were laughing again outside. Every detail seemed like a metaphor. The crack in the flower vase, the clouds before the sun, the solitary chestnut tree outside the window. The heating clicked, and I jumped. My suit felt too tight.

There were photos in an open drawer of the desk. I picked a few of them up. One showed my wife, myself, and Charlotte as a girl; it must have been fifteen years old. I stroked Charlotte's face and slipped the photo into my jacket pocket. In the bottom left-hand drawer I saw a heavy yellow envelope with a yellow wax seal. Underneath it was a medical report and covering letter.

Forensic medical report

RE: Injuries sustained by Charlotte Maria Farewell; possible administration of GHB

History

Ms. Farewell reported that she had been to a party the previous evening and had been drinking alcohol. She woke up the next morning in a field. She reported having no memory of how she had got there, and as both her underpants and her tights were bloodstained, she feared that she had been raped. Ms. Farewell complained of pain in her lower abdomen.

Forensic examination report

Ms. Farewell is 170 cm tall, weighs 71 kg and is right-handed. She was alert, fully oriented, and appeared psychologically normal.

Forensic evidence obtained

Swab of bite mark, gelatine lift of bite mark, vaginal introital swab, anal swab, cervical swab, cheek swab sample for comparison, blood and urine samples for chemical and toxicological testing.

Evaluation

At the time of examination, the nineteen-year-old Ms. Farewell was observed to have blunt force trauma injuries to her face, arms and buttocks. The injuries to the left side of her lip were probably caused by the impact against her teeth. According to the examining clinician, the injury to her left nipple was probably a bite. The red circular marks around her wrists indicated that an implement was probably used to immobilize her. She had extensive bruising on both buttocks caused by blunt force trauma. This is likely to have been inflicted by blows from a blunt object.

The gynecological examination found deep tears in the mucous membrane at the entrance to the vagina, indicating penetration with an object.

A pretest for seminal secretion using a PSA SemiQuant test gave a positive result on the hair and was negative on the other samples. The semen of at least two men was detected. Further molecular genetic tests are necessary. We are requesting permission to carry out these tests.

The chem-tox analysis (see separate test report) gave no indication of alcoholization or the influence of medication or narcotics at the time of examination. No trace of GHB

in the urine. This does not rule out the
administration of GHB, however, as it is
usually only detectable in the blood for up
to 6 hours, or up to 12 hours in urine.

I took the envelope with our yellow seal from the drawer. It was empty.

Charlotte returned to the flat that evening. I heard her before I saw her. I was sitting in the chair by the desk, still holding the envelope.

"I'm one of them," I said, before she could speak. "I'm a Butterfly."

She saw the envelope in my hand. When she spoke I could barely understand her; her voice was thick with tears.

"Why didn't you protect me?" she asked.

I looked at her, my daughter: her blonde hair reminded me of my late wife. Deep inside me I felt something shatter.

"I'm sorry," I said. I couldn't ask for her forgiveness.

I left the flat. I couldn't put my finger on what had just happened, but I knew that life as I knew it no longer existed. Outside on the pavement I collided with a young Asian man in a Pitt Club tie. He looked a bit like a clown. I was shocked when he shoved me aside and bawled in my face, "Watch out, old man!"

I didn't respond. I sat down on the pavement outside Charlotte's house and leaned against her door. I lowered my

197

head until the long, silvery blond hair of which I'd always been so proud fell forward across my face.

I disgusted myself.

Josh

Monday morning: a walk by the river, watching the rowers training. I'd recently started going for walks like these; they bored me, but I thought it was very stylish, going for walks on my own. Low-intensity activity is good for your health. And I'd seen Stichler jogging on his own and thought: *maybe I can be the boxer who always goes for walks on his own.* I'd like it if people said that about me. Strong story.

I watched the Clare College eight glide past. The team were all rowing in time. I'd always admired this harmony. I thought it was a retarded sport, and those one-piece suits were mega-gay, but I liked the calm atmosphere in the boat, which was only made possible by the subjugation of the self. Stichler and I were like that, too: We'd joined forces, we'd been like two rowers in one boat, even though we'd boxed in different weight classes and at different times. We'd won that fight together. I did find it pretty weird the way Stichler behaved at the Club, wanting the minx all to himself, but it was kind of funny too, watching this little bloke carry her off. We laughed for ages after he left. That was what I was thinking about that morning. Along with something I'd recently read: that horses are apparently incapable of crying out in pain, which was a fascinating notion, especially when you applied it to people.

Early that morning I'd called the bank where I would be doing my internship and asked if I could name a different person to be contacted if anything should happen to me. The bird on the phone sounded a bit confused, but she noted down the name "Hans Stichler." Boom.

A few minutes later I got a message from Stichler. Coincidence, presumably. He wrote that he would wait for me in the University Library, south wing, fourth floor, next to the bookshelves marked NA – NAV.

I seldom went to the University Library, a hideous building in the west of the city with a tower like a monstrous erection. In my first term a friend had told me that a complete collection of British pornographic literature was hidden in this tower. I'd checked it out, and was embarrassed that I'd believed the story.

Stichler was standing between the shelves, running the back of his hand along the spines of the books; with anyone else it would have looked camp, but with him it looked cool. He seemed different: he was wearing jeans, a hoodie and trainers, and he hadn't shaved for a few days; the stubble was a greenish shimmer on his skin. Such a fit bloke. Maybe I could try out a beard like that; I'd never thought of it before. It wasn't his outward appearance that made Stichler seem different, though; he came across as exhausted, yet somehow alert. His handshake was firm and a little longer than usual.

"Sorry I ruined the evening," he said.

"Hey, no probs. You wanted the gold minx all to yourself; I get it."

We went down to the Reading Room. It was thirty-six feet high, and a warm light fell through the arched windows along the tops of the walls. Library attendants made sure no one spoke. The air smelled of book dust. I worried about the moisture balance of the mucous membranes in my nose, but the smell drove me agreeably wild. Sometimes glued books smell fantastically like pussy.

Stichler sat at a table and went to pull up another chair, accidentally knocking it over. One of the library attendants immediately shushed him. Cambridge was so ridiculous.

He took a piece of white paper and a fountain pen out of his bag. I smiled when I saw that. When I was a child I used to sit at a desk writing for hours just to observe my own handwriting. I'd wanted to see how much I could change it, and I was proud of it.

Stichler unscrewed the cap of his fountain pen.

Do you know why I took the girl with me? he wrote.

"Why don't we just talk, mate?" I whispered. The bastard library attendant raised an eyebrow.

Stichler tapped his forefinger on the sentence he had written.

Do you know why I took the girl with me?

Yes, I wrote, in blue ink and round letters. I handed the pen to Stichler. Our fingertips touched.

Why? he wrote.

I smiled to myself. I really liked this crazy guy.

It was your night, I wrote.

Stichler looked at the piece of paper for a long time, rotated it slightly, and frowned a little. We heard the pages of books being turned. A young woman was tapping on her laptop keyboard at a nearby table.

You have interesting handwriting, Stichler wrote.

No one apart from my teachers had ever commented on this. Stichler really was different. Maybe we could train together in Cornwall over the summer.

I took the pen and made an effort to write nicely.

Thank you, my friend, I wrote. I added a decorative flourish to the tail of the first *y*. Boom.

Stichler screwed the cap on the fountain pen, stood and picked up the paper, and we left the Reading Room. We wandered around a bit more between the bookstacks. I thought I'd like to go to the library more often in future. All that peace and quiet: sweet. The air was less dry in the upstairs rooms. I took a book about flambéing off a shelf, sniffed it, and lost myself in its pages. When I looked up again Stichler had disappeared. I'll write to him this summer, I thought. I wanted to write and tell him that I didn't actually like butterflies because they reminded me that they had once been caterpillars. Stichler was sure to appreciate that.

Billy

My parents' house in Richmond smelled of warm yeast that morning, of starched cotton tablecloths, Penhaligon's fragrances, scented candles at eighty pounds apiece, of oranges, gin, and old money.

I sat at the breakfast table with my mother. I'd come home because she'd made crumpets, which she didn't often do any more. She'd sent a car to Cambridge to fetch me. The cook had spooned the jams into white porcelain bowls, and the crumpets sat beside them in a basket. In the middle of the table was a serving tower laden with French cheeses. Mother was choosy when it came to cheese; she insisted one could only eat cheeses from the Auvergne.

She told me how a few days ago a man had rung the doorbell and said he'd seen our kitchen from outside. He worked for a film production company and was looking for a house for a location in the new *Bridget Jones* film. Our kitchen was perfect, he said, with the stove kitchen island and the glass roof. He'd need the house for a month, during which our family could live at the Savoy, and we'd receive a five-figure sum in compensation. Mother had thanked him politely, given his visiting card to the butler who stood by the door, and gone to tennis.

The crumpets were good. I'd missed them. I was wearing my Blues blazer, my hair was freshly washed and tied back. Mother stroked my arm; she said how proud my father was of me, and that he sent his best. Clearly his pride had not been sufficient to ensure his actual presence. He'd gone in to work early, Mother said. Something to do with a pipeline in Nigeria that he had to take care of.

"It's pathetic, I know; his son's home for a visit and he's taking care of a pipeline."

We talked a bit about our summer holiday. I wanted to go to Colombia but Mother thought it was too dangerous; she'd rented a couple of bungalows in Barbados instead, which she said was bad enough. Perhaps my German friend from the boxing team would like to come out for a week.

I smiled, remembering how I'd realized Hans was lying. It was at the hospital. I may have been drunk, but I'd seen the name the nurse wrote on the form. I'd been surprised, but I'd pieced together a story the end of which I couldn't figure out. I knew the feeling, though: Sometimes it was just easier to pretend to be someone else.

On our last day together, when we were sitting on the fountain in the marketplace, Hans had asked me a question I'd been thinking about a lot ever since.

"What is truth?" he'd asked.

I'd said nothing at the time because I didn't know the answer, and that bothered me somehow. Now it occurred to me that it had sounded almost as if he were saying goodbye, and I wondered whether I would ever see Hans again.

"What is truth?" I asked my mother.

She spread a little lemon curd on her crumpets.

"The truth is that my crumpets have turned out very well," she said.

She smiled, told me I should stop racking my brains about such nonsense and eat the crumpets instead. I took her hand and gazed at her blue veins and the gold ring with the blue stone. Mother gave me a serious look, and set her mask aside for a moment. I loved this about her; she was a bit like me, but the other way round. All day long she played the fine lady, who drank tea at Fortnum & Mason and purchased her lingerie at Rigby & Peller, but I knew that this was just her way of making life bearable.

"The truth, Bill," she said, "is the stories we keep telling ourselves until we believe they're the truth."

Then her smile was back again. It was perfect. Perhaps it was from her that I'd learned to play the game.

I looked up from the table; the sky hung low and gray over the glass roof. The light blue of the blazer almost looked pretty against the color of the clouds. I wondered if it was too early for a gin and tonic. Mother would understand. I nodded to the butler standing in the corner and ordered my drink with two slices of lemon.

"For the vitamins," I said.

Mother laughed and said I absolutely must try the lemon curd. The lemons were from the Amalfi coast; they were particularly flavorful this year.

Hans

I was woken by a chambermaid sticking her head around the door of the hotel room. Rays of sunlight fell across the empty mattress and rumpled bedclothes beside me. A brown, unlined notebook lay on the bedside table. I'd spent a long time writing in it the previous evening.

The flagstones on the balcony were warm beneath my feet as I stepped out, carrying Charlotte's laptop, and sat down in the morning sun. I was naked, wearing nothing but the red gold necklace. I balanced the laptop on my knees.

On the website of a major British newspaper I read the story about the Butterflies. The paper had published everything I'd told Alex. She'd noted every little detail. The photo accompanying the article was of the yellow wax butterfly seal. The word "bloodstained" did not appear in the text. All the men named had either been uncontactable or had refused to comment on the accusations. Angus Farewell, too, had remained silent. These men should be considered innocent until proven guilty, wrote the author. At the end of the article stood the names of the current Butterflies. One of them was Hans Stichler, the man who, for a short time, I had been.

I showered, put on a vest and the jeans I'd been wearing all week and went downstairs in my bare feet. It had been

Charlotte who suggested coming here. She wanted to get away from it all, she'd said.

We'd flown to Verona, rented a little car, and driven down the west bank of Lake Garda. I'd sat at the wheel with Charlotte alongside, her feet on the dashboard. She'd said she couldn't drive on the right; she wound down the window and held her hand out into the wind. I'd been amazed at how relaxed she was.

In Gardone Riviera she'd asked me to turn right and stop in front of a pink marble villa. Mussolini and his lover had lived there, Charlotte said, waiting for the end of World War II. Now it was a hotel. She paid for a week in advance. The taps in the bathroom were gold.

That morning I walked across the terrace and sat on the jetty. It smelled of warm wood and seaweed. A waitress in white gloves brought me an espresso; a fresh roast of Kenyan beans, she said, floral with light grapefruit notes. All I could taste was coffee. I dunked the sweet almond biscuits and enjoyed it.

Sitting in the sunshine I ran through the events that had brought me here one more time. I thought of the Cambridge men who had seen me as someone I was not.

Billy had spoken to me before I'd possessed a tie in the right colors. I wondered how I would explain to him that the life he'd thought was mine had been a lie. Billy would understand, though. Friends do.

I thought of Alex, too, sometimes. It kept occurring to me that the first time I met her in Cambridge she had asked me, "You still box, don't you?" She'd known all along that the Butterflies had something to do with the boxing club, but she couldn't have known it from Charlotte, because Charlotte had no memory of the Butterflies. It seemed monstrous, but I could only think of one explanation. I knew that Alex had been at Cambridge forty years ago. So had Angus Farewell. She had told me that she "sort of" knew him. I recalled the look on her face.

That morning I made a promise to myself. It seemed important, and was actually quite simple: I would never lie again.

Charlotte had known for a week now that her father was part of the same group as her abusers. Shortly after our departure he sent her a long e-mail in which he swore that he had never hurt any woman, and would do everything in his power to prove his innocence. Charlotte should ask me about it, he said; we'd discussed this subject only recently, and the fact that he was worried about the way things were going with the Butterflies. I told Charlotte that this was true.

We were already at the hotel on Lake Garda when Charlotte got the e-mail from her father. She was lying beside me while I wrote in my diary, and when she spoke she broke the silence.

"I'll only get through this if you stay with me," she said.

When I gave her the piece of paper Josh had written on in the library, she nodded immediately. All the same, I asked her to compare the word "night" on the paper with the word "night" in the Butterflies' letter, which I'd brought with me. The writing was identical. Charlotte folded both pieces of paper and threw them in the wastepaper basket by the bed. She asked me what that person was called. I'll never forget how she said the words "that person." I said Josh's name. She typed it into her phone. I was glad she didn't speak of it any further.

I watched Charlotte swimming in the lake. The reflection of the sun on the water was so bright it blinded me. She'd swum out too far. For a moment I was worried about her. I didn't know whether she would ever get over all this.

She came out of the water, sat down beside me on the jetty and put an arm around my shoulders. Her skin was wet and cold. The scar on her chest from the rabbit scratch was a little paler than usual. Probably the cold, I thought.

"Do you think they have badminton racquets here? Maybe we should do something to help us think about nice things. Do you fancy a game?" she asked.

I took her fingers and kissed her wrist. I'd meant to kiss the back of her hand, but I missed. I knew it didn't bother her, though. Which was one of the reasons why she was the one.

She looked as if something was glowing inside her.

"No. I don't," I said.

I looked out over the lake. The old man who owned the hotel had told us the previous evening that there was a shack up in the village where the vintners' sons sometimes boxed.

Alex

At six in the morning I got up, went to the corner shop and bought the newspaper. I read the cover story about the Butterflies once, quickly, all the way through, then again, more slowly.

Angus

Night, soft soles, black clothing.

I entered the house through the servants' entrance, which wasn't locked. Apart from the kitchen, all the rooms were dark. I'd been watching the place for a week and had waited until only Josh Hartley, his grandmother and the cook were at home. I knew that Hartley's room was on the second floor, facing the sea, and that at this hour he was almost certainly asleep.

One month earlier I'd received a postcard on which was written, in Charlotte's hand: *The person who did that to me is called Josh Hartley.* I burned the postcard in the garden. The reverse was a photo of the Old Town in Verona. The flames flickered blue and red.

My lawyers advised me to sue the paper that had accused me of being a rapist, and to do nothing else. The Butterflies were gone, but it was never just the name that made them powerful. There would always be a network, as long as the University of Cambridge existed and as long as men aspired to power.

I'd done everything right. That, at least, was what I felt, and that was precisely what I couldn't bear. I had lost my daughter, and when I received her postcard I knew what a father had to do in this situation.

I disassembled the falling block rifle, cleaned and lubricated it, wrapped the parts up separately and packed them in a suitcase. Then I hired a car and drove to Cornwall.

I opened the door to Hartley's room. Moonlight shone through the slats of the blinds. Hartley was lying in bed, asleep. I saw a pair of boxing gloves on the writing desk, and beside them a photograph of him arm in arm with Hans Stichler. The shotgun weighed five and a half kilos. The man who sold it to me called it "the elephant killer." Hartley's body was covered by the duvet. Only his head was visible, and one pale hand, hanging over the edge of the bed.

Hans

I was with Charlotte when the policeman called. She put her phone on speaker. The policeman said he was very sorry, that they didn't like to break news like this over the phone.

The only witness they had been able to question was the cook, who'd been on the ground floor. She'd said the shot had been so loud she'd dropped the bowl in which she was whisking lemon juice, butter, egg yolk and sugar. She'd been planning to serve Josh a lemon tart with his tea the following morning; he was so fond of it. When the cook had heard the shot she had climbed into the cupboard under the sink, and that was where she was crouching when the second shot rang out.

The policeman said he'd never seen anything like it— the effect of a large-caliber rifle fired at close range. As if the shooter had wanted to erase every memory in both their heads.

The policeman's reconstruction of the crime had led him to the following conclusion. Angus Farewell must have snuck into the house, gone up to the second floor, put the gun to the young man's forehead as he lay in bed and pulled the trigger. He had then loaded a second cartridge, removed one shoe, positioned the rifle with the stock on the ground and the barrel between his teeth, and pressed the trigger with the big toe of his right foot. It was an extremely long shotgun. With the barrel in his mouth, not even a very tall man would be able to reach the trigger with his hands. The policeman said he had himself performed a reconstruction with a broomstick, to make sure.

The motive was unclear. The only clue was a photo. The policeman had found it in the shooter's left jacket pocket. It showed Angus Farewell, a woman, and a blonde child with curly hair.

Someone, presumably the shooter, had written something on the back of the photo. It said: "All of it is true."

CENT 09-10-2020